The first thing Tom noticed when he and Jo got in from school that afternoon was Jo's badge.

'What's that?' he said.

'A badge,' said Jo.

'It says *Form Captain*!'

Tom's voice was accusing; as if she had no right to be wearing a badge which said *Form Captain*. As if, perhaps, she had stolen it from someone or picked it up in the gutter on her way home.

'You can't be form captain!'

'Why can't she?' said Mrs Jameson.

'*Her*? *Form* captain? It's got to be a joke!' said Tom.

Pride prevented Jo from speaking. She longed to say, in the cold and crushing tone it was sometimes necessary to adopt with Tom, that it was not a joke but perfectly serious – except that, of course, would be a lie. And while Jo hadn't the least objection to telling the occasional untruth when the circumstances demanded, Tom would only sneer and jeer all the more when she came home badgeless tomorrow evening.

Bossyboots

Jean Ure

RED FOX

A Red Fox Book
Published by Random House Children's Books
20 Vauxhall Bridge Road, London SW1V 2SA

A division of Random House UK Ltd

London Melbourne Sydney Auckland
Johannesburg and agencies throughout the world

First published by Hutchinson Children's Books 1991

Red Fox edition 1993

Text © Jean Ure 1991

Printed and bound in Great Britain by
Cox & Wyman Ltd, Reading, Berkshire

ISBN 0 09 960790 5

BOSSYBOOTS

1

'The nice thing about the summer term –' Fij swung her bag, exuberantly, as she and Jo turned into Shapcott Road – 'the really *nice* thing is that we get to do cricket.'

'And the really *nasty* thing –' that was Bozzy, bleating piteously from behind – 'is that we have exams.'

'Oh, exams.' Fij dismissed exams. Exams weren't important: cricket was.

'They're not for months, anyway,' said Barge, stumping along in her solid Bargelike fashion next to Bozzy. Barge never believed in crossing her bridges till she came to them. 'Live for today is *my* motto.' She was full of these original remarks. 'What is the point of working oneself into a frazzle over something which may never happen?'

'Exams do happen,' said Bozzy.

'Yes, but not necessarily to you . . . who knows *what* might not occur between now and then? You might fall through a crack in the paving stones or get chicken pox or drop head first into a vat of boiling oil or – well! Almost anything. You really must learn,' said Barge, bracingly, 'to look on the bright side.'

Jo giggled.

'It's all very well for you,' said Bozzy, 'you're not going to come bottom of everything and get Rude Remarks written all over your report. . . . Do you know,' she enquired, doing a couple of little skips to catch up with Jo and Fij, 'what Miss Lloyd actually had the nerve to write under *General Comments* last term?'

'No,' said Jo. 'What?'

'She wrote, *I sometimes seriously wonder whether Chloë removes her brain and leaves it at home every day.*'

'Cheek!' marvelled Fij, at the same time as Barge's voice boomingly declared, 'We all wonder that.'

'Yes, and you can go and bury yourself!' screeched Bozzy. You would never have guessed that Barge and Bozzy were best friends.

They walked on up the road, the four of them abreast. It was strictly forbidden to walk four abreast: 'It is not good manners,' Miss Lloyd had curtly informed them, last term, 'to take up the whole of the pavement. Kindly remember that you are Peter High girls and act accordingly.'

Peter High, properly known as Petersham & St Mary's High School for Girls, had a reputation for being one of the best-behaved schools in the borough, even better than Daneshill, which was independent.

('That's because we're all *girls*,' Jo had boasted to her brother Tom, but Tom had only stuck his fingers in the air and made a rude noise.)

'Fathead!' said Bozzy, biffing Barge with her bag.

'Popeye!' retorted Barge, biffing Bozzy with her hip.

It was all quite amiable. Barge and Bozzy had a whole range of insults which they exchanged purely as a matter of routine. Back in September at the beginning of the school year, Jo had really thought they hated each other, but she had grown used to it by now and scarcely noticed any more. It was when they started threatening to

2

garrotte each other or to shove each other's teeth down their throats that you knew trouble had begun. Until then, you could safely ignore it.

'Pig face,' said Bozzy.

'Turnip features,' said Barge.

'Lovely weather,' said Fij conversationally to Jo, 'for the time of the year. Don't you think?'

'Oh, absolutely,' gushed Jo. 'Just right for the first day of term.'

'I'm dying to play cricket,' said Fij.

'Me, too,' agreed Jo. She had spent the whole of last week practising her off drive with her older brother, Andy. (Not with Tom: Tom jeered at the thought of girls playing cricket. That was because Tom was only thirteen and an idiot. Andy was sixteen and sensible. Even Jo, at twelve and a bit, was more sensible than Tom.) 'I suppose Nadge will be games captain?' she said, wistfully.

'Bound to be. Who else is there?'

Jo didn't like to say, 'Well, there's always me,' even though she had an older brother and had been practising her off drive. Nadge only had a little sister; you couldn't practise off drives with eight-year-olds. But Nadge was extra super brilliant where games were concerned. She was always made captain. It would seem colossal cheek on Jo's part to go pushing herself forward, especially as she was one of the ones who had transferred from other schools, whereas Nadge, along with Fij and Barge and Bozzy, and Gerry Stubbs and the Lollipop, and one or two others, had all come up from the Homestead, which was the junior department of Peter's. It still gave them a slight edge over the new girls.

'New girls,' Barge had once loftily informed Jo, 'only stop being new girls when they've been here a year.'

Jo had a whole term to go before she stopped being a new girl. She couldn't be made captain of anything this time.

'It's a question,' said Fij, bowling an imaginary ball at an oncoming bus stop and stabbing a passing Second Year in the eye as she did so – 'Do you mind,' snarled the Second Year. 'That was my eye!' 'Yes, and it was *my finger*,' retorted Fij, with feeling. There was no love lost between First Years and Second Years. 'It is a question,' said Fij, tenderly massaging her fingertips, 'of who is going to be vice captain.'

'I shall vote for you,' said Jo, loyally. Fij was her special friend. Out of school she was best friends with Matty, because Matty lived next door and she and Matty had been friends since Juniors. But at school Matty was best friends with Jool, while Jo was part of the famous Laing Gang.

The Laing Gang were: tall skinny Fij (known as Fij on account of her full name being Felicity Isobel Jarvis); big bellicose Barge, officially down in the register as Margery Laing but mostly referred to as Barge for obvious reasons; little Bozzy (Chloë Boswood) with her stumpy blonde plaits and bulgy blue eyes, all busy and bustling and self-important; and Jo herself, Joanne Jameson, known as Jo to her family, Jammy to her friends.

At Juniors, where there had been no fewer than three Joannes – Big Jo, Medium Jo, and Little Jo – she had been Jo in the middle, and that, sometimes, was how she still thought of herself: as a *middling* sort of person.

4

Middling tall, middling-looking – brown hair, brown eyes (just like loads of other people), round squidgy face with a few blobby freckles ('A bit like a squashed apple,' as Bozzy had once cordially informed her) – middling good at games, middling good at lessons. On her last term's report, under the dreaded *General Comments*, Miss Lloyd, their form mistress, had written: *Jo is a rewarding and responsible member of the community though has yet to learn to temper enthusiasm with restraint. On the whole, a good all-round performer.*

In other words, thought Jo, *middling*. Perhaps one day she would manage to distinguish herself.

They continued on their way up Shapcott Road, part of a steady stream of girls in the red blazers and blue-checked dresses which were the summer uniform of Peter's. Barge and Bozzy, still trading insults – 'Pasty face!' 'Collywobble!' – were jostling each other on and off the pavement. Fij, wielding an imaginary cricket bat like a giant fly swatter, was slashing imaginary cricket balls to the boundary, Jo skipping and hopping at her side. It had to be said that with the four of them strung out in a row it didn't leave very much room for anyone else who might wish to make use of that particular bit of pavement. In fact it didn't leave any room at all, but that still didn't give Gerry Stubbs the right to shout abuse at them from the other side of the road.

'Oy! You lot! Walk properly!'

'Well, honestly!' fumed Barge. 'Who *does* she think she is?'

Bozzy gave a little flounce, in defiance. 'She's not form captain *yet*.'

'No, but she soon will be.' Fij said it glumly. Gerry

5

Stubbs had been voted form captain for as long as anyone could remember.

'Was there ever a time when she wasn't?' said Jo.

The others thought back, to their days in the Homestead.

'No.' Bozzy stated it positively. 'She's always been. There isn't anyone else bossy enough.'

'There's Barge,' said Jo, before she could stop herself. 'That is,' she added, hurriedly, 'not that Barge is *bossy*, precisely. I'm not saying that she's *bossy*. But she is the sort of person that people sort of – well, take notice of.'

'That is one way of putting it,' said Fij. 'I suppose.'

Barge preened. 'People do take notice of me. I'm what is known as a natural leader. One either is or one isn't. To give you an example,' said Barge, happy as always to be talking of herself, 'I told my brother the other day that if he didn't buzz off and stop messing with my things he'd get what was coming to him. He stopped *immediately*.'

Barge's brother was six years old. He wasn't even a quarter the size of Barge.

'You've either got it or you haven't,' said Barge. 'You can't force people to do what you tell them. With me they just seem to do it quite willingly. It's just a knack I have.'

'So why don't we vote for Barge?' said Jo, brightly.

There was a pause.

'What did you say?' said Fij.

'I said, why don't we vote for Barge?' said Jo. 'As form captain, you know.'

'Vote for *Barge*?' shrieked Bozzy. 'Are you crazy?'

Fij stopped slashing cricket balls. She turned, slowly, to look at Jo out of grave grey eyes.

'I don't think that would be a very good idea,' she said.

No; neither did Jo now she came to consider it. Gerry might be unbearably autocratic, but Barge was a bully. If you didn't stand up to her she rolled right over you and left you squashed flat.

Barge tossed her head. 'Pray don't concern yourselves on my behalf!' ('Didn't know we were,' said Bozzy.) 'I can assure you wild horses wouldn't pin a form captain's badge on *me*.'

'Age-old custom,' hissed Fij, behind her hand, to Jo. 'In the Homestead . . . we always used to drag in a couple of wild horses to pin badges on people.'

Barge's big square face turned a purply colour. 'It would be gratifying –' she addressed the air in front of her – 'if one could, just occasionally, converse with those who understand English in its more advanced forms . . . semaphores, smileys, that kind of thing.'

(Jo thought, but could not be sure, that Barge was talking of metaphors and similes, which they had done with Miss Lloyd in English last term.)

'It would make a nice change,' said Barge, 'that is all. However, to return to the subject in hand, I can assure you I have absolutely no desire to become the craven lackey of authority. Form captain, in other words,' she explained for Bozzy's benefit.

'Mind you,' said Fij, 'almost anything – apart from Barge – would be better than Gerry.'

'She's got so she takes it for granted,' grumbled Bozzy. 'As if it's hereditary, like being the Queen or something.'

'It might actually do her good if someone else *did* get in for once.'

7

'So long as it wasn't anyone tedious and boring, like Pru.'

Prunella Frank was Gerry's best friend. They usually took it in turns to come top of exams.

'What we need,' said Barge, 'is someone who could see the funny side of things and can't keep order for toffee.'

Bozzy giggled. 'You mean like Jammy, for instance.'

Jo put a hand to her heart in a mock swoon. 'Spare me!'

'Oh, don't worry,' said Barge, kindly. 'Miss Lloyd would never let anyone like you be form captain . . . You have to be the right sort of person.'

'Unfortunately,' said Fij.

'If Gerry gets in *again*,' said Bozzy, 'I shall blow a wotsit.'

'Well!' Barge gave a superior little titter. 'That's enlightening!'

'What's a wotsit?' said Fij.

'Oh! You know . . . a wotsit – a thingummy.'

'Tantrum?'

'*No*! One of those things that you blow.'

'A trumpet?'

'*No!*'

'A gasket?' said Jo.

'*That's* it,' said Bozzy. 'A gasket! I shall blow a gasket.'

As they turned in through the school gates Fij said, 'What *is* a gasket?' but nobody knew.

'It won't stop me from blowing one,' said Bozzy.

2

There were four houses at Peter High: Nelligan, Roper, Sutton and York (named after four of the school's earliest Head Mistresses). Forms were divided up according to House, and each House had its own colour. Nelligan, or Nellie's, was light blue, Roper was red, York yellow ('yuck yellow') and Sutton green.

'*Pea* green . . . green with horribly slitty-eyed envy.' Barge said it with relish as she and the gang made their way to 1N's form room on that first morning of the summer term. The Laing Gang were all in Nellie's: Sutton was their greatest rival. 'You just wait,' said Barge. 'We'll thrash them to a pulp! Grind them into the mud! Annihilate!'

She was referring to the end of term, when the year's House points – both pluses and minuses – were added up and the winner awarded the Dorothy Beech Cup (given to the school by the parents of Dorothy Beech, who had died tragically but heroically driving an ambulance in the First World War).

Sutton had won the Cup for the last five years, so it was certainly time *someone* thrashed them. It would be pleasant if it could be Nellie's, but Jo didn't hold out much hope. Every class in the House, from First Year up to Third-Year Sixth, made its contribution to the overall total; and thus far, it had to be said, the contribution coming from 1N had been pretty dismal.

When it came to *work*, they could hold their own with anyone: Gerry Stubbs, Pru Frank and Naomi Adams carried off almost all the honours. They didn't just vie for top place in 1N, but for top place in the whole of the year. On the sports field it was a fairly even battle between Nellie's and Sutton: Nellie's had Nadge, but Sutton had Lee Powell (who happened to be Nadge's best friend). Everyone agreed that Nadge was more gifted, but Lee made up for it by being the more aggressive. Nadge could never get terribly worked up about actually winning, though for all that Nellie's had done well. 1N had more than contributed their share of house points for both games and work. Unfortunately, they had more than contributed their share of order marks, as well.

Order marks were given for bad behaviour and for rule breaking, and it did seem, looking at the record, that 1N were worse behaved and broke more rules than most people.

'But it would be *awfully* boring,' said Fij, 'to be perfect.'

'Oh, awfully,' agreed Jo.

'Imagine if we were all like – well!' Fij lowered her voice. 'Like Gerry, for instance.'

They fell silent, contemplating Gerry as she walked ahead of them down the main corridor. Gerry never did anything wrong. She was one of those maddening people who seemed constitutionally incapable of getting into trouble. She was about Jo's height, but rather more solid, with dark hair cut neatly into her neck (not flying about all over the place like Jo's) and a face which might have been carved from a block of granite: handsome but forbidding. You knew at once that Gerry was responsible, dependable, and above all, *bossy*.

'It wouldn't be so bad,' said Barge, 'if she had any sense of humour, but she hasn't. None whatsoever. Not even the tiniest little shred. . . . Do you remember that time in the Homestead when we brought plastic maggots to school and put them in her dinner? She didn't even *twitch*, let alone laugh.'

'Did she scream?' asked Jo, with interest. 'I would have done.'

'No, she just said, "Who's been childish enough to put plastic maggots in my dinner?" You can't have any fun,' grumbled Barge, 'with a person like that.'

At that moment, Gerry turned. She must have sensed their presence or maybe heard their voices. (But hopefully, thought Jo, not what they had actually been saying.)

An expression of distaste crossed Gerry's face. 'It's you lot again! You *know* you're supposed to keep single file in the corridors.'

'Not on the first day back,' said Bozzy.

'First day back hasn't anything to do with it! Rules are still rules.'

'Pish to the rules!'

Gerry's face darkened. 'You'd better not let a member of staff hear you say that.'

'Why?' said Bozzy, insolently. 'What's it to you? You're not form captain yet.'

'And may not be, either,' added Barge. 'So there!'

'Oh, for goodness' sake!' said Gerry. 'Do you have to be so infantile?'

She turned, witheringly, and marched off down the corridor ahead of them.

'You can tell she's rattled,' whispered Fij to Jo.

'Absolutely,' said Jo, though for the life of her she couldn't imagine what Gerry had to be rattled about. She must be as aware as the rest of them that she was the only person fit to be form captain. Barge was too pushy, Fij not pushy enough; Nadge, though easily the most popular person in probably the whole of the First Year, habitually broke every rule in the book and didn't care tuppence for good behaviour; and there simply wasn't anybody else with the necessary authority. Gerry was quite safe.

They were surprised, when they reached their form room, to find a prefect waiting for them instead of the familiar figure of Miss Lloyd, with her beautiful blonde hair and lingering fragrance of flowers. 1N were immensely proud of Miss Lloyd. She was by far the best of all the First Year form mistresses. She wasn't an old bag like Mrs Denver, or a fright like Miss Pollard, and she didn't try to be super-trendy like Ms West, whom Sutton thought was so marvellous and wonderful. Imagine having a form mistress who wore miniskirts! Miss Lloyd dressed *properly*, as a teacher should, in long swirly skirts and silk blouses, or sometimes dresses, but always smart and elegant, not in the least bit frumpy.

'Old-fashioned!' sneered the mob from Sutton's; but they would. No one took any notice of that crew.

'Where is Miss Lloyd?' demanded Fij, worried.

'Miss Lloyd has had to go off in a hurry to visit her mother in hospital. She'll be back tomorrow. In the meantime –' the prefect glared at them defiantly – 'you'll have to make do with me.'

'Who is she?' hissed Barge, in Jo's ear.

'Don't know.' Jo had seen her around the school – sitting in assembly with the other prefects, doing point duty in the corridor – but their paths, so far, had never crossed. She wasn't a member of the drama society, nor in any of the games teams. She looked, decided Jo, uncharitably, like a nobody: shapeless and ungainly, with a sacklike body, and round pink specs perched on a pointy nose in an utterly forgettable face framed in utterly forgettable mousy hair.

Bozzy, who had been squinting sideways at a briefcase laid on top of the desk, self-importantly reported her findings: 'It says Proline Marsh.'

Barge looked at Jo. '*Proline*?'

Jo shrugged. If people could be called things like Parthenope and Robina – which two girls at Juniors *had* been – there seemed no reason why they shouldn't be called Proline.

'Well!' Barge could be quite broad-minded when she set her mind to it. 'I suppose it takes all sorts.'

Up at the front of the class, Proline Marsh cleared her throat. It sounded nervous. 'Could you all find your-selves a place, please, and sit down.'

There was a moment's hesitation, then a sudden mad scramble for desks. For the last two terms Miss Lloyd had insisted on their sitting in alphabetical order. It just so happened that alphabetical order separated the worst of the talkers and gigglers from the other talkers and gigglers. Left to themselves, 1N promptly gathered talkers and gigglers into one big bunch, thus:

Jo Fij	Bozzy Barge	Emma Sally Gilmore Hutchins (The Bookends)
Matty Julie Ann McShane Gillon	Melanie Ashley Peach Wilkerson	Gerry Pru Stubbs Frank
Claire Nadia Kramer Foster (Nadge)		Naomi Laurel Adams Bustamente

The whole of the back row were talkers and gigglers, and the second row likewise until you came to Gerry and Pru. Nadge, who talked and giggled practically nonstop and was the most disruptive of the lot, was admittedly next to Claire Kramer, who was too self-sufficient (and bound up in her ballet) to either talk *or* giggle, but Nadge could be a disruptive influence wherever she sat.

'Hey! Jool!' Bozzy leaned across from her desk and prodded Julie-Ann Gillon. Julie-Ann turned, with a shriek.

'Ow! Who's poking me?'

'Anyone poking you has me to answer to . . . We're the Black Faction!' announced Matty. 'Me, Jool and Nadge . . . Hey, Nadge!'

Nadge also turned. Matty, copying Lee Powell, raised her fist in the Black Power salute. Nadge instantly did likewise.

'Shuddup!' Jool made a chopping motion. 'We don't want none of that!'

'Yes, we do . . . gotta support the cause, man!'

14

'That's racist!' yelled Melanie.

'Who says?'

'I do!'

'Well, up yours!' said Matty. 'Honky,' she added. It was a word she had picked up from Lee Powell.

'*Honestly*,' said Ash.

Bozzy, meanwhile, in the midst of the hubbub, had passed a screwed-up twist of paper, torn from the edge of her rough book, for Jool to pass to Nadge. Nadge unscrewed it, read it, and stuck up a thumb, her little Siamese-kitten face alight with mischief. Bozzy leaned in to whisper to Barge, who nodded and leaned across to the Bookends.

'Please!' Proline beat a hand, ineffectively, on the desk. 'Please will you all stop making such a noise!'

Gerry stood up. 'Everybody BE QUIET!'

The noise stopped, as if by magic.

'Thank you.' Proline subsided weakly on to her chair. Jo wondered why it was she who had been chosen to look after them rather than one of the other prefects – Michelle Wandres, say, or Elizabeth Grey, the House games captain, or her friend Wendy Armstrong. Any one of them could have kept order quite easily, Elizabeth because she was heavenly, Wendy because she was forceful, Michelle because she was power crazed. This poor mutt didn't stand a chance.

'Now,' said Proline, 'if you're all settled –'

'I'm not!' cried Emma Gilmore, one of the Bookends. 'I'm not settled!'

Proline looked flustered. 'Why not? What's the matter?'

'I don't know,' said Emma. 'But I don't *feel* settled.'

15

Nadge bounced about on her chair. 'P'raps what you need is a walk round the room.'

'Yes!' Emma sprang up, delighted at the suggestion. 'That's exactly what I need . . . a walk round the room! To relax me, you know.'

'Shall I come with you?' said Sally Hutchins, known to one and all as the Mouse. 'I better had,' she said to Proline, 'in case she gets lost.'

'I'll lead the way!' That was Nadge, taking advantage of the situation. (Nadge could rarely manage to sit still for more than five minutes at a stretch.) 'Ta ra, ta ra!' tootled Nadge, blowing an imaginary trumpet.

In front of Proline's helpless gaze, 1N erupted from their desks and set off on a noisy parade up and down the gangways. Only Gerry Stubbs and her mealy-mouthed minions, Pru and Naomi, remained seated. Even Claire, giggling, was prancing along in the rear doing ballet steps.

'*Please*,' begged Proline. 'Please, everybody!'

'*Oh, the elephant patrol*,' sang Nadge (*The Jungle Book* had been showing during the summer holidays),

> '*Is a question rather droll,*
> *As we stamp and crush*
> *Through the underbrush*
> *To our military goal –*'
> '*TO OUR MILITARY GOAL!*'

The rest of the form joined joyously in the chorus. Fat Lollipop made braying noises, Claire did an elephant dance. Proline's pale face was covered in red confusion. Jo could see the beads of perspiration breaking out on her forehead. Just for a second she felt sorry for her; and then she thought, 'She's a *prefect*.' Prefects shouldn't be prefects if they couldn't keep control.

Gerry suddenly pounded on her desk lid. 'Sit down! Everybody . . . SIT DOWN!'

'Why?' said Nadge, pertly.

'Because I say so!' roared Gerry.

'And who,' Barge demanded of the room at large, 'does she think she is when she's at home? The Prime Minister?'

'You're not form captain *yet*!' shrieked Bozzy, growing over-excited.

'If you people don't do as you're told,' cried Proline, clutching at straws, 'I shall tell Miss Lloyd!'

The threat had the desired effect: 1N ceased their cavortings and returned, albeit by the longest and noisiest routes possible, to their desks. In spite of smelling of flowers and wearing gorgeous clothes, Miss Lloyd was quite capable of turning nasty. It didn't do to cross her – specially not on the first day of a new term.

'Right,' said Proline, wiping a limp hand across her forehead. 'Let's get on. I'm going to take the register first, then we'll elect monitors, then you can fill in your timetables. Then –' she glanced at her watch – 'it should be time for assembly.'

The taking of the register went off quite smoothly, apart from the Mouse not responding to her name because (or so she claimed) she had forgotten that it *was* her name.

'It's true! It's true!' A chorus of voices hastened to lend their support. 'She does forget! She's been Mouse for so long she thinks it's her real name!'

'What was it again? What was it I'm really called?'

'Sally Hutchins.'

'That's me?'

'I think so,' said Emma. 'Unless it's someone else. Is there anyone else here who answers to the name of Sally Hutchins?'

'Look,' said Proline, growing desperate, 'is it you or isn't it?'

'Yes, it is,' said Gerry, grimly. There was going to be trouble in store, thought Jo, if Gerry was voted form captain again. And how could she not be? Who else was there? No one!

'Melanie Peach – Geraldine Stubbs – Ashley Wilkerson.' Proline closed the register with obvious relief. 'Now we'll elect monitors. Let's start with games. Someone propose a name and someone else second it.'

'What's sekendit?' said Bozzy.

'*Second* it. The *name*.'

Bozzy looked blank. 'What name?'

'She just told you,' said Melanie. She giggled. 'Sekkon Ditt!'

'Who's Sekkon Ditt?'

'Sarah Sekkon Ditt!'

'I don't know anyone c –'

'The name of the person who's been proposed, for goodness' sake! How old are you people? Stop messing around and get on with it!'

'We don't do it this way,' said Barge.

'What do you mean, you don't do it this way?'

'We don't do what you said . . . all this proposing and second-itting.'

'So what do you do?'

'We just shout out names and you write them on the board and then we vote. That's the way we do it.'

18

'Oh, all right.' Proline wasn't going to argue. She groped in Miss Lloyd's desk for a piece of chalk. 'So who wants to suggest someone?'

Fat Lollipop said, 'Nadge.'

'*Nadge*?'

'Nadia Foster,' said Gerry.

Nadia Foster, wrote Proline, in what Jo privately considered to be rather childish handwriting for a sixth-former. 'Anyone else?'

The Mouse suggested Fij, Matty suggested Jo. Bozzy suggested Pru Frank and everyone giggled because Pru was the world's worst when it came to anything physical. The final voting was:

Nadge	 14
Fij	 1
Jo	 0
Pru	 1

Jo was a bit hurt to think that someone had actually voted for Pru, even if only as a joke, rather than her. They voted again for vice captain and of course it was Fij.

'Now form captain,' said Proline. She stood, with chalk poised.

Naomi said, 'Gerry Stubbs.' A barely suppressed groan ran round the back of the class. From where she sat, Jo could see Gerry's face grow white and clenched. Then, from the front row, Nadge made a suggestion which Jo couldn't quite hear.

'Gemma?' said Proline.

Jo giggled. 'Gemma,' she whispered. She nudged at Fij. 'Who's Gemma?'

'Not Gemma,' said Nadge. 'Jammy.'

Proline looked at her suspiciously. So did Jo.

'Jammy's not a name,' said Proline.

'Jo Jameson!' yelled Bozzy.

Gerry, with a frown, suggested Pru again: Pru, with another frown, suggested Naomi. When it came to voting, Jo couldn't immediately decide what to do. Seeing her own name up there, in the running (not that she was really) seemed to have knocked her brain sideways. She supposed she really ought to vote for Gerry except that Gerry really had become so unspeakably bossy. Naomi, on the other hand, would be quite useless, she was far too reserved; and Pru, although forceful, scarcely ever spoke to anyone save her intellectual equals. Jo dithered so much that in the end she didn't vote for anyone at all, a fact which Proline seemed not to notice.

Only two people voted for Gerry: they were Pru and Naomi. Only one person voted for Pru: that was Gerry. Nobody at all voted for Naomi. That left twelve people to vote for Jo.

'So that's Jo Jameson, form captain,' said Proline, 'Gerry Stubbs, vice captain. OK, everyone! Timetables.'

She seemed not to have the least idea that Class 1N had just started a revolution.

3

'1N –' Miss Durndell, the Head Mistress, was reading from the list of monitors which had been handed to her just before assembly. 'Games captain, Nadia Foster; form captain, Joanne Jameson.'

An audible flutter ran round the ranks of the First Years, down at the front of the hall, as Jo scrambled to her feet and scurried up the steps after Nadge on to the raised platform where Miss Durndell stood at her lectern with the three rows of prefects seated in a semi-circle behind her. Several heads turned, slyly, to look at Gerry and see how she was taking it, but Gerry sat stiff and straight-backed, staring directly ahead. Gerry had her pride. She wasn't giving anyone the satisfaction of letting them know that she cared.

Jo supposed that she *did* care; she would, if she were Gerry. To be ousted, after all these years, by a mere new girl! It almost made Jo feel guilty, because surely the form could only have voted her in as a joke. They couldn't seriously believe she was the stuff of which form captains are made. None the less . . . she squinted down at the badge which Miss Durndell was pinning to the front of her dress: blue, for Nelligan, with the words *Form Captain* printed in gold letters. It was an honour, whichever way you looked at it.

'Put the flags out!' screeched Bozzy, tearing into the

playground at break. 'The Dictator has been deposed! We're free! Hurray!'

Gerry was only a few paces behind; she must have heard, thought Jo, worried.

'I'm ever so sorry I didn't vote for you as games captain,' confided Fij. 'I would have done, 'cause I knew Nadge would get in anyway, but I was scared in case you got in as vice captain and then Miss Lloyd might've said you couldn't be form captain as well. Not, of course,' she said hastily, 'that I *knew* you were going to be form captain. But it did sort of cross my mind.'

Jo remembered, now, the note which Bozzy had passed to Nadge. So it was a put-up job! They had all been in it together!

'We had to do *some*thing,' said Fij.

'*Any*thing,' said Bozzy, 'to get rid of the Dictator.'

Gerry looked at Bozzy long and hard; so did Pru and Naomi.

'It's what is known as a bloodless coop,' said Bozzy.

'Coup.' Jo muttered it, feebly. She didn't like the way that Gerry and her henchwomen were glowering at them. If looks could have frozen, the Laing Gang would have been turned to ice by now.

'Coo?' shouted Bozzy. 'You mean like in, *coo* we're liberated?'

Bozzy was showing off; even Barge obviously felt it to be in bad taste.

'The enemy has fallen,' she said. 'There is no need to gloat. And in any case,' she added, as Gerry & Co. moved out of earshot, 'it might not be diplomatic.'

'Diplomatic? Pooh!' said Bozzy.

'You won't say diplomatic pooh when the Dictator is back in power and throwing her weight around.'

22

'What?' Bozzy stared at her, eyes popping. 'What do you mean?'

'What I mean,' said Barge, 'in plain simple English such as I would hope even a cretin would be capable of understanding, is *gather ye rosebuds while ye may*.'

There was a pause. Even Jo wrinkled her forehead.

'Pardon?' said Bozzy.

'Granted,' said Barge.

Bozzy turned, in perplexity, to Jo. 'What,' she said plaintively, 'is she on about?'

Jo shook her head.

'What I expect she means,' said Fij, bracingly, 'is that we can have a good time *this* term but when Gerry gets back into power *next* term –'

'Who says she's going to get back into power? I'm not going to vote for her again!'

'Well, and neither am I, probably, but –'

'Listen, you dumb idiots!' shouted Barge. 'Must I use words of one syllable? *Watch my lips*. . . . A short life and a merry one. The condemned man ate a hearty breakfast. GATHER YE ROSEBUDS. . . . You don't imagine for one moment, do you, that Miss Lloyd is actually going to let someone like Jammy stay on as form captain for a whole *term*?'

Bozzy's face fell. 'But we voted for her!'

'Only as a joke.'

'You mean –' Jo swallowed, wondering why she felt as though someone had just kicked her in the stomach. 'You mean tomorrow, when she comes back, she'll make Gerry captain again?'

'Well, she is almost bound to,' said Barge, 'isn't she? You must admit, no one could really take you *seriously*.'

23

'No.' Jo said it humbly. 'I suppose not.' It was only what she herself had already thought, but somehow it still hurt. Fij squeezed her arm.

'I'm sure she'll let you be vice captain.'

'Fat lot of good that'll do!' wailed Bozzy. 'Did you see the way Gerry was looking at me?'

Fij giggled. 'Not surprised, after some of the things you said!'

'Just because I'm more honest than the rest of you . . . just because I always speak my mind. . . . Oh! Help me, someone! What shall I do?'

'Try looking on the bright side,' advised Barge, briskly. 'Just think, by this time tomorrow you could have fallen under a bus.'

'Or Gerry could,' suggested Fij.

Bozzy cheered up. 'I suppose that is always a possibility.'

'And in the meanwhile,' said Barge, 'we must all eat hearty breakfasts and make hay while the sun shines.'

'Thought we were going to gather rosebuds,' muttered Jo. It was silly, she *knew* it was silly, to feel disappointed. Common sense should have told her that of course Miss Lloyd wouldn't let a flibbertigibbet creature such as herself stay on as form captain. It wasn't even as if she had ever wanted to be form captain. But now that she was . . .

'Let's go and do something *absolutely forbidden*,' said Barge. 'Think of something!'

They all thought; all except Jo. Jo was thinking, I don't really want to do something absolutely forbidden. Not, at any rate, while she was still wearing her form captain's badge.

'I know, I know!' Bozzy bounced, self-importantly. 'Let's go and ring on Mr Dobbs's door and run away!'

Mr Dobbs, the caretaker, lived in a small cottage adjoining the Homestead. The Homestead was several yards further up the road from the Senior School: it was absolutely forbidden for pupils to leave the premises during school hours without permission.

'That's a good idea!' said Barge.

'Why? Why is it?' Jo hopped after her, anxiously, as Barge began striding out across the playground. 'What are we doing it for?'

'We are making hay,' said Barge, 'while the sun still shines. . . . Once the Dictator is restored we shan't be able to even *breathe*, hardly.'

But so long as it was only Jo, they could do whatever they felt like doing, even if it was something absolutely forbidden. (And pretty silly, as well.) I'm just a puppet, thought Jo, trailing dismally in the others' wake; just a figurehead. She plucked at Fij's sleeve.

'Do you think we ought?' she said.

Fij thought about it. 'Well, probably not,' she said, 'but it is a gesture. I think it's important to make gestures from time to time.'

They slipped out of the playground by one of the side doors. Jo thought, I don't know why I'm doing this, but that wasn't being strictly honest. She did know why she was doing it. She was doing it because the others were doing it and because she was too much of a coward to stand against them. It was true, she *wasn't* fit to be form captain.

The only solace was that Mr Dobbs's cottage, when Barge went charging up to the front door and punched at

25

the bell, whilst Fij and Bozzy stood holding open the gate for a quick get-away, turned out to be empty. At any rate, no one came to the door, which was just as well since Bozzy in her excitement managed to trip over her own feet and go sprawling.

'Oh, bliss!' sang Barge, as they erupted back into the playground just as the bell was ringing for the end of break.

'Where have you been?' said Gerry, suspiciously.

'Striking a blow for freedom!' shrieked Bozzy.

Gerry narrowed her eyes. 'Don't forget the House meeting,' she said, pointedly, to Jo.

It was just as well Gerry had reminded her because otherwise Jo almost certainly would have forgotten. The House meeting, which 'all elected officers will be expected to attend', was held in the lunch break, in the Senior Library (Sutton's were holding theirs at the same time, in the Sixth Form Common Room). Jo felt a fraud, taking her place amongst all the genuine, properly elected officers. Martha Prince and Katy Wells, from the Second Year, didn't trouble to hide their contempt.

'Really,' said Katy, 'the First Years are just *too young* to be treated as responsible human beings.'

'The sort of people,' agreed Martha, 'who would go out and vote for a pop star as Prime Minister.'

'So what if we did?' said Nadge. 'Couldn't be much worse than what we've got at the moment, could it?'

Martha sniffed. Katy said, 'Fat chance we stand of winning the cup *now*.'

All Second Years, as a matter of course, loathed and despised all First Years; all First Years, as a matter of course, loathed and despised all Second Years. It was a feud going right back to the days of the Homestead. Katy and Martha had nothing personal against Jo; but still it was discouraging.

'Don't want to take any notice of those gawkers,' said Nadge. 'I think it's a great gas!'

The House was addressed first by Kay Wyman, who was the House captain, then by Elizabeth Grey, who was games.

Kay spoke for about two minutes. She was a remote, rather aloof person, said to be incredibly brilliant. She reminded them that this was the term when the Dorothy Beech Cup was awarded, and that 'we must all work together to get as many points as possible – and fewer order marks, *please*, than some of us contributed last term.'

Kay and Martha both turned pointedly to look at Jo and Nadge. Jo's cheeks obligingly fired up, but Nadge only pulled a face and stuck out the tip of her tongue. Martha sniffed again, and Katy said, 'First years!'

Elizabeth then stood up and addressed them, in ringing and passionate tones, for almost a quarter of an hour on the subject of games. Elizabeth was rumoured to be almost as brilliant as Kay, but while Kay had once been overheard to remark that she considered most 'so-called' sports to be barbaric and never turned up at matches if she could possibly avoid it, Elizabeth played and studied with equal enthusiasm and vigour. She was everybody's favourite prefect.

'In conclusion,' she said, smiling across at Jo and Nadge (sucks to the Second Years) 'I'd just like to welcome the First Years to their very first season of cricket and remind them that here in Nellie's we have a long tradition of fielding strong teams. So . . . I shall be looking forward to seeing you in the nets and hope that we shall be able to recruit at least one or two of you for the Under-14s. I'm sure we shall!'

Jo instantly determined that if she did nothing else that term she was going to be chosen for the Under-14 cricket XI.

On the way down from the library, Nadge said, 'We'll have to have a form meeting.'

'Mm.' Jo nodded. They always had a form meeting after a House meeting, but since by the time it was arranged she probably wouldn't be form captain any more, it was difficult to show the proper amount of interest. 'When?' she said, trying.

'Tomorrow? In the lunch break?'

By tomorrow lunch break she *certainly* wouldn't be form captain any longer. Miss Lloyd was due back tomorrow morning.

'Where?' said Jo, still struggling.

'In the form room; it's far the best place. Do it in the cloakroom and they come and chuck you out, do it in the playground and there's people eavesdropping all over the place.'

'Don't we need permission to use the form room?' said Jo, vague stirrings of responsibility awakening within her.

'Oh! Don't need to bother about that. After all, it's official,' said Nadge.

They still needed to ask permission – but what did it matter? By the time of the meeting it would be Gerry's problem, not Jo's.

*

The first thing Tom noticed when he and Jo got in from school that afternoon was Jo's badge.

'What's that?' he said.

'A badge,' said Jo.

'It says *Form Captain*!'

Tom's voice was accusing; as if she had no right to be wearing a badge which said *Form Captain*. As if, perhaps, she had stolen it from someone or picked it up in the gutter on her way home.

'You can't be form captain!'

'Why can't she?' said Mrs Jameson.

'*Her*? *Form* captain? It's got to be a joke!' said Tom.

Pride prevented Jo from speaking. She longed to say, in the cold and crushing tone it was sometimes necessary to adopt with Tom, that it was not a joke but perfectly serious – except that, of course, would be a lie. And while Jo hadn't the least objection to telling the occasional untruth when the circumstances demanded, Tom would only sneer and jeer all the more when she came home badgeless tomorrow evening.

'I think Jo will make a very good form captain,' said Mrs Jameson, meaning well but only making matters worse.

'Wait till I tell Robbie!' said Tom.

Evil. Tom was *evil*. 'Don't you say anything to Robbie!' shrieked Jo.

Robbie Wyngarde was Jo's boyfriend – well, sort of boyfriend. Her dad teased her about it, but her mum said she was too young to have boyfriends and that Robbie was just a friend who happened to be a boy. He also, unfortunately, happened to go to Tom's school and to be in Tom's form.

29

'*I*'ll tell him,' said Jo, 'if I feel like telling him.'

'Why?' said Tom. 'What's so secret about it?'

'There isn't anything secret. I just don't want you telling him.'

'In which case,' said Mrs Jameson, 'he won't. Will you?' She looked hard at Tom. He humped a shoulder.

'Don't see why not.'

'Because your sister doesn't want you to! Isn't that good enough reason?'

'S'ppose so.'

'Well, then . . . promise her!'

'Promise,' mumbled Tom.

Jo knew that he would keep his promise. Tom was as mean as could be, but he never cheated.

After supper they all went into the back garden, the whole family, and played cricket, using Andy's bat and a tennis ball. Even Jo's mum had a go, though she hadn't played cricket at school and wasn't sports-minded like the rest of the family. Andy said Jo had the makings of a 'very useful middle order batsman'. Even Tom, after she had twice hit him to the boundary (that is, as far as the wall at the end of the garden) stopped making his rude remarks about girls playing cricket.

'Might get together sometime and do some fielding practice,' he said.

Next morning, Jo went in to school with Matty. Yesterday morning she had met up with the Gang, but that had been a special arrangement just for the first day of term: she and Matty had been walking to school together since Juniors.

'Great about you being form captain,' said Matty. 'Should have some fun this term.'

Miss Lloyd was back, wearing a long red flowery skirt and a crisp white blouse (which would stay crisp the whole day, unlike any white blouse which Jo ever wore). On the board, in Nadge's big sprawly hand, was a notice: HOUSE MEETING 12.30 *IN HERE*. EVERYONE TO COME. *By order* Nadge and Jam. Miss Lloyd glanced at it and didn't say anything, but after assembly she called to Jo to stay behind as the others left for the Home Ec. room.

This is it, thought Jo. She almost felt like removing her lovely blue badge right there and then. Why wait to be asked? Why not just do it? Get it over with?

'Well, now,' said Miss Lloyd, pleasantly. She gestured towards Nadge's notice. 'I take it you have asked permission to use the form room?'

Jo's cheeks blushed peony scarlet. 'Um – er – n-not exactly,' she said.

'Not exactly?' Miss Lloyd's tone was still pleasant but Jo knew, from experience, that it could change in an instant. 'What does that mean? Exactly?'

'It means – um – well . . . it means – what it means,' said Jo, growing desperate, 'because of you not being here and it being official and – um – one thing and another,' said Jo, 'we never sort of – um – got around to it. As it were.'

'But you were going to, I trust?'

'Oh, yes,' said Jo. 'Absolutely. Yes. We were just sort of – waiting. As it were.'

'For me to come back.'

'Well – yes. And to sort of – get settled in.'

'Very considerate of you,' said Miss Lloyd.

Jo's cheeks blushed ever brighter. She wished she felt

31

brave enough to ask Miss Lloyd how her mother was, which would, after all, only be polite and show that she cared – because she *did* care – but somehow the moment didn't seem quite right.

'On this occasion,' said Miss Lloyd, 'I will believe you. But in future, if for any reason I'm not around, go and get permission from someone else. Rules may at times seem irksome, but I can assure you they are not made without good reason. Not, at any rate, in this establishment. The reason behind this particular rule, for instance, is really very simple. We are responsible for you and we need to know at any moment of the day where you are. Imagine if a fire broke out and no one knew that you were in here. I would assume that you were in the playground, would I not? Where you are meant to be.'

Jo nodded. She didn't like to point out that in fact Miss Lloyd would have known they were in the form room because of having read Nadge's notice. It would almost certainly come under the heading of impertinence. Miss Lloyd was reasonable, but only up to a point.

'Now,' said Miss Lloyd. Jo's heart went thumping down to her shoes. This was the moment! She might just as well tear the badge off straight away. 'You've been elected form captain,' said Miss Lloyd. 'That is a great responsibility, and responsibility is not always easy. However, I am expecting good things of you; you have the ability, if you care to use it. I'm hoping that you will. Any problems, don't hesitate to come to me. All right?'

Jo gaped. 'You mean –'

'Mean what?'

'You mean I can s-stay as form captain?'

'You were elected, weren't you? It's not up to me to interfere in the democratic process. What are you trying to do? Get me lynched?'

Jo grinned, a trifle sheepishly; and then, on impulse, before her courage could fail, she said: 'H-how is your mother?'

'As well as can be expected,' said Miss Lloyd. 'She's a very old lady.' She smiled. 'But thank you for asking.'

Jo skipped off, after the others, to a double period of Home Ec. This was going to be a *good term* she thought.

4

'Hey! Guess what?' It was Nadge, mischief-making as usual, who went bounding up to Robbie at the Youth Club on Friday evening. 'Guess who's been made form captain!'

'You?' said Robbie.

Nadge gave a mad cackle and jerked a thumb over her shoulder. 'Your girlfriend!'

'Jo?' said Robbie.

Jo's cheeks instantly started on their peony routine. She had extracted a promise from Tom, she had warned Jool and Matty (on pain of death), and the Gang were no problem because they lived too far away to come to the Club. The one person she had forgotten about was Nadge.

Nadge gave another of her mad cackles. 'You've only got the one girlfriend, haven't you? Or haven't you? Hey, Jam! Hear that? He's got a whole harem!'

Now it was Robbie's turn to blush. Jo felt embarrassed for him. She could happily have bashed Nadge over her curly head with a table tennis bat. She would have told Robbie in her own good time, preferably when they were on their own, without an audience of gawpers and gigglers. Jool was the worst. She went into paroxysms at the least little thing (you could stand up and recite pages from the telephone directory and have Jool rolling about the room in hoops).

'Jammy!' she tittered. 'Form captain!'

Robbie, bravely (because he was still blushing) looked across at Jo and said, 'What's so funny about it?'

Jo shrugged a shoulder. It wasn't for her to say.

'J-Jammy!' Jool was almost at her last gasp: the whole thing was so exquisitely humorous. 'Jammy . . . f-form captain! O-o-o-h! I shall die laughing!'

'See, it was a joke,' explained Matty.

'But why is it funny?'

'Well, 'cause last term Jam got just about more order marks than anyone else, almost.'

'I didn't!' Jo was moved, indignantly, to protest.

'Got more'n I did,' said Matty.

'And more'n I did!'

'I didn't get nearly as many as Nadge,' said Jo.

'Oh, well! Nadge!'

Nadge grinned.

'*And* I didn't get as many as Barge or Bozzy.'

'Yeah, well . . . them two.'

'And they were only for talking, mostly, in any case,' said Jo. Talking in assembly, running in the corridors, swinging off the hot-water pipes in the downstairs cloakroom. . . . 'Nothing really *bad*.'

'Not like me,' said Nadge. She rolled her eyes. 'I am really *bad*. Miss Lloyd said so.'

'*Did* she?' said Jo, sidetracked.

'On my report. She said, *Nadia could be a considerable asset to the school community if she could only learn to moderate her bad behaviour*.'

'Sounds as if they should've voted you for captain,' said Robbie, 'if they'd really wanted a joke.'

Jool squeaked and clutched podgy hands to her ribs.

'Nadge is games,' said Jo.

'Yeah, and anyway –' Matty said it very seriously – 'they would've known then we were just messing about. With Jam they're not quite sure. They think it's just we're fed up of the Dictator.'

'Who's the Dictator?'

'Gerry Stubbs. She's horrible,' said Jool, wiping her nose on the back of her hand. 'What's your one like?'

'Our form captain?'

'Yeah.'

'We don't call them form captains at Milden Hall. We call them head of class.'

'So what's he like? Your one?'

Robbie hesitated. The blush had come back to his cheeks. He looked really sweet, thought Jo, when he got bashful. But what was he getting bashful *about*?

'Who is your head of class?' said Nadge. 'Anyone I know?' Nadge was one of those people who seemed to know everybody. 'It's not that Keith Barber, is it? He'd be really *gross*.'

Keith Barber had once been Tom's best mate. Robbie shook his head, so that a lock of hair fell into his eyes. (*Blue* eyes.) Jo loved it when it did that.

'So who?' said Nadge.

'Well, it's – um – me,' said Robbie. 'Actually.'

'Tom never told me that!' cried Jo, indignantly.

Trust Tom. Fancy keeping a thing like that from her.

'Are you bossy?' said Nadge. 'Hey! Tom!' She flapped a hand at Tom across the room. 'Is Rob bossy?'

'You'd better believe it!' yelled Tom.

'You want to watch it,' said Nadge. 'Know what happens to bossy form captains?' She whipped a finger across her throat.

'I bet he's not as foul as the Dictator was,' said Matty. 'Honest, it was like having Mrs Thatcher in class. Always keeping on at you . . . nag nag nag, nitch nitch nitch. Never a moment's peace.'

'Jammy's great,' said Jool. 'She just lets you alone.'

'Yeah.' Matty nodded. 'We can do what we like with Jam.'

It was later in the evening, when they were playing a game of sardines in the churchyard outside and Jo and Robbie were crouched together behind the gravestone of William Thomas Trellis 1882–1975 ('Still a boy at 93') that Robbie whispered, 'Do you really let them do whatever they want?'

'Well –' Jo was cautious. 'Not all of the time.' It would be too wet to say that she let them do whatever they wanted *all* of the time, although in fact that was what it amounted to. 1N simply didn't take any notice of Jo when she tried to exercise control. They had elected her for fun, and fun was what they were determined to have.

Yesterday, for instance, after the lunch break, Jo had come back to the form room to discover books still on desks, a pair of trainers in the gangway, the remains of Mrs Stanley's Maths lesson still on the board.

'Who's tidiness monitor?' she'd demanded.

'Who's tidiness monitor?' had squawked Jool, in imitation, and everyone had giggled. Jo had stood her ground.

'Who *is* tidiness monitor?'

'Who *is* tidiness monitor?'

'Oh, now look here,' had said Jo.

'Oh, now, look here!' had squawked Jool.

In the end, in desperation, Jo had cried, 'You know what happened on Tuesday!'

On Tuesday Michelle Wandres, doing a prefects' inspection, had awarded them an order mark 'for the perfectly foul state of your room'. Even that reminder hadn't sobered them up.

'Pish to order marks!'

'Pish to prefects!'

'Pish to tidiness!'

Jo had gone off to look at the form notice board.

'*Matty*!' She had turned, accusingly. '*You're* tidiness monitor!'

'Well, knock me down with a feather!' had said Matty, and they'd all dissolved again. Only Gerry, very pointedly, in grim silence, had left her seat and started collecting up the offending items. Jo had helped her. She hadn't said anything to Matty at the time, but on the way home after school she had tried reasoning with her.

'You don't want to take it so seriously,' had said Matty. 'Just 'cause you're form captain . . . It's only a *joke*. No one expects you to do anything.'

'Are you very strict?' whispered Jo to Robbie, as they crouched together behind their gravestone.

Robbie grinned. 'Like Mrs Thatcher.'

She looked at him, doubtfully, not sure whether he was teasing. 'Do they actually do what you tell them?'

'They do when I come on heavy.'

'But doesn't it –' Jo took a breath. 'Doesn't it make you unpopular?'

'Haven't noticed,' said Robbie. 'Anyway, they voted for me, they knew what they were getting.'

That was the difference, thought Jo: Robbie had been

voted for because they thought he would make a good head of class. She had only been voted for as a joke. Nobody was going to listen to anything she had to say.

'Thing is,' said Robbie, not at all in a preachy way, but almost apologetically, 'there doesn't seem much point being elected if you're not going to do anything.'

Jo knew that he was right; but who wanted to be unpopular? And anyway, it wasn't fair: *she* hadn't asked to be form captain.

On alternate Wednesdays the first period after lunch was private study under the supervision of a prefect. Last term the prefect had been Wendy Armstrong. Everybody had groaned, because Wendy was strict and wouldn't put up with any nonsense, but at least they had all got on with their work. This term, it seemed, they were to be looked after by the Prole. (The Prole was Bozzy's nickname for Proline Marsh; it had quickly caught on.)

Jo could sense, right from the start, that 1N were going to play up. The Prole could obviously sense it, too, or perhaps everyone always did play up when she was in charge. She was tense and pale and kept pushing her glasses back up her nose with the first finger of her left hand.

The first thing Jo noticed was when a giggle ran along the back row and she looked up to see one of the Bookends, Emma Gilmore, who also wore glasses, also pushing them back up her nose with the first finger of her left hand. Seconds later and Jool and Fat Lollipop were doing it as well. Jo leaned forward and poked Jool in the back. Jool sprang round, giggling.

'Stop it!' hissed Jo.

'Stop what?'

'Doing what you're doing!'

'What am I –'

'Joanne Jameson!' snapped the Prole. 'I saw that! You can come out here and sign the order mark book.'

Jo's cheeks flushed scarlet with humiliation. The Prole was an *idiot*. She deserved to have people make fun of her if she couldn't even recognize when the person wearing form captain's badge was doing her best to rescue her.

'If the order mark's for talking,' said Jool, boldly, 'then I ought to have one as well.'

'It is not for talking, it's for cheating.'

Cheating? Jo's mouth opened wide in indignation. Words failed her.

'Asking people to help with your homework is a form of cheating.'

'But I wasn't!' said Jo.

'So what were you doing?'

'She was telling me to stop doing this,' said Jool, shunting like mad at her glasses.

The Prole flushed.

'She was,' said Jool. 'Honestly.'

'I see.' The Adam's apple in the Prole's throat suddenly shot up and hit her chin. She gulped, and swallowed. 'Well. All right. I really don't see what business it is of yours, Joanne –' absolute *idiot* – 'but I'll accept your word that you weren't cheating. Go and sit down and get on with your work.'

'What about the order mark?' said Jo.

'I'll let you off this time, but be warned.' Without

thinking, the Prole pushed at her glasses. Barge and Bozzy promptly collapsed. 'Any more of this behaviour,' said the Prole, 'and I shan't hesitate.'

An eruption of giggles ran through the class, bursting out pop pop pop! like an attack of chickenpox from desk to desk. The Prole lowered her head over her books and did her best to pretend it wasn't happening. Jo, scarlet-cheeked, plumped herself down again next to Fij. So much for trying to exercise authority. Fat lot of good it had done her. From now on, as far as she was concerned, the Prole could fight her own battles. Jo wasn't coming to her aid any more.

For the next few minutes there was comparative peace. The spectacle wearers grew tired of shunting their spectacles up and down, and even Barge and Bozzy, contentedly playing their own private games of consequences, managed to do it without too much obvious nudging and giggling. Jo, with relief, concentrated on Geography homework for Miss Briarley.

Agricultural belts of the Mississippi Basin, she wrote. *1) Spring Wheat and Dairying*. How horribly boring Geography was!

She became aware that Fij was craning over, pointing with her pen at Mississippi and raising a questioning eyebrow as she did so. Jo nodded, vehemently. She mightn't be much good at Geography but she did know how to spell. Fij frowned and pointed at her own book, where she had variously written Mississippi, Misissippi, Mississipee. Jo shook her head. Fij sighed. She had just scored a line through Mississippi, Misissippi, Mississipee and was about to try again when Matty reached behind her with one hand and deposited a scrap of paper on the desk. Fij hauled it towards her, turning it sideways so that Jo could read it at the same time. On the scrap of paper were the words, *When I cough count 3 then drop your books on the floor. Pass this on. Nadge.*

Before Jo could stop her Fij had obediently passed the note across the gangway to Bozzy. There was nothing Jo could do. (And anyway, why should she? It was only the Prole.) Already, silently sniggering, Bozzy had leaned forward to tap Melanie on the shoulder. Melanie pushed the note to Ash, Ash sent it back to Barge, Barge passed it to the Bookends. The Mouse then screwed it up and lobbed it over the heads of Gerry and Pru on to the desk of Fat Lollipop. The Lollipop bumped round in surprise. Proline looked up.

'What's going on?' she said. 'Get on with your work!'

The Lollipop plucked at the note and unfolded it. A big happy beam spread itself across her face.

I can't do anything, thought Jo. Not even Robbie could do anything to prevent it if the whole class decided to play up.

Jo bent her head over her Geography. *Very similar to the prairies of Canada*, she wrote.

Down at the front of the class, Nadge coughed. Jo found herself counting, bracing herself for what was to come. One – two – three – CRASH!

It even took Jo by surprise, and she was ready for it. Poor old idiot Prole almost leapt out of her skin.

'What –' she gripped the sides of the desk with white-knuckled hands – 'what was that?'

The class took up the cry.

'What was it?'

'What was it?'

'Help, somebody! Do something!'
'Ring the bell –'
'*Do* something!'
'Clear the room! It could be a bomb!'
'A bomb!'
'It's a bomb!'
'*Do* something!'
'Call the police!'
'Ring the fire alarm!'
'Get an ambulance!'
'Do something!'
'*Ow*!'
'Do you mind?'
'You idiot!'
'What?'
'That was my *eye* –'
'Well, move it!'
'*Do* something!'
'Shelter! Take shelter!'

With a bloodcurdling screech, Nadge hurled herself to the floor and curled up in a ball beneath her desk. The Lollipop tried to copy her and got stuck. The Bookends cracked their heads together and started punching, Bozzy overturned her chair, Barge overturned her desk. Fij lay prostrate in the gangway, Jool and Matty flung themselves into each other's arms, exaggeratedly screaming, whilst Melanie flew into the stationery cupboard, hotly pursued by Ash. (Ash always did what Melanie did. She had no mind of her own.) Even Claire entered into the spirit of the thing, snatching up her school bag and sticking her head in it.

The only people not participating were Gerry and her

faithful followers, and Jo. This time last term Jo would have been at the forefront. She would have been there with Fij, rolling in the gangway, acting terrified even as they giggled together. Today, because of her blue badge, she knew that she couldn't. There were definite disadvantages to being form captain.

Gerry looked at her across the room. It seemed to Jo that the look was contemptuous. Gerry would never have let them behave like this. If Gerry had been form captain they would have been too *scared* to behave like this. Gerry mightn't have been popular, but at least she was respected. But who wanted to be unpopular? And anyway, thought Jo, a trifle sullenly, it shouldn't be up to the form captain. It was up to the person in charge. That was the Prole. It was up to her to put a stop to it. Couldn't she exercise *any* authority?

The Prole was on her feet, nervously twisting an elastic band between her fingers.

'Stop it!' she said. 'Stop it this instant! You're all being very silly and childish. If you don't s –'

At this point, the elastic band snapped. Jool and Matty shrieked, Melanie slammed the cupboard door, Barge raced for the fire extinguisher.

'Margery!' The Prole's voice rose, high and thin, above the hubbub. 'Leave that alone!'

The door opened and Elizabeth Grey appeared. She paused on the threshold, coolly surveying the scene.

'Playing war games?' she said.

Barge turned and beat a quick retreat back to her overturned desk. Claire removed her head from her bag and began busily shaking the bag upside down as if in search of something. Melanie emerged, sheepish, from the stationery cupboard, with Ash sidling after.

'Taken up residence?' said Elizabeth.

Melanie gave her a beatific smile. 'Just looking for mice,' she said.

'Mice?' said Elizabeth.

'Well, or mouse . . . mouse in the stationery cupboard. Eating up the stationery. Yum yum yum,' said Melanie, making what she evidently thought were mice-eating noises whilst at the same time plucking at her lips with wriggling fingers.

'I see,' said Elizabeth. 'And what is Felicity doing on the floor? Having a fit, or did your legs give way?'

'No, no!' Airily, Fij picked herself up. 'I was just practising my yoga.'

'In private study?'

'Yes, well, you see, I am doing a project on it,' explained Fij, improvising rapidly. 'I wanted to find out what the – ah – lily, that is lotus, position felt like done on a hard surface.'

'Painful, I should imagine.' Elizabeth said it drily. She turned to a now red-faced Prole. 'I'm sorry barging in on you like this but I wanted a quick word with Nadia. Is she not here?'

'Yes.' The Prole nodded, weakly, in the direction of Nadge's desk.

'Oh! There you are!' said Elizabeth, as Nadge came cheerfully crawling out on hands and knees. 'And what are you doing a project on? Contortionism?'

Nadge grinned, cheekily. 'I thought the mouse from the stationery cupboard was down there.'

'Ah! So that's where it went,' said Melanie. Melanie not only had an uncle who was an actor in a TV soap but had her own pretensions to being an actress. She could

45

never resist capping other people's lines. 'There we were,' she said, 'hunting high and low. Weren't we?' She turned, chattily, to Ash. 'High and low all over the place. In the chalk, in the –'

'Thank you, Melanie. That will be quite enough. If I were you –' Elizabeth spoke crisply – 'I should save your dramatic talents for the stage. They leave one rather cold in real life. Nadia, just come outside with me a minute, will you? And I'll have a quick word with you, Gerry, while I'm –' Elizabeth stopped. She was looking at Gerry, and seeming puzzled. Then her face cleared. 'I was forgetting!' she said. 'You're form captain this term, aren't you, Jo? I'll have a word with you, then, while I'm here.'

Heart thudding, Jo followed Nadge out of the room.

'All right,' said Elizabeth. 'Just very briefly. I won't keep you. . . . Nadia, we're having a special meeting to organize the interhouse rounders after school this evening. We've only just arranged it. Will you be able to come? Good! I was hoping you would. It is quite important. OK, back you go, then. See you at three-thirty. Now, Jo. I don't know what was going on in there just now, but whatever it was it didn't look much like private study; more like some kind of an orgy. You're lucky one of the staff didn't come along or you'd have been booked for heaven knows how many order marks. Do, please, have a word with your lot and remind them that we are hoping to have a stab at the Cup this term. That kind of behaviour simply is not on – and I shall hold you responsible for making it clear to them. You are, after all, form captain.'

It was so unfair. It was so un*fair*!

Jo trailed back into the classroom with her cheeks aglow. Just because the Prole couldn't keep order! People shouldn't be prefects if they couldn't keep order.

Somewhere inside her a small voice made itself heard, suggesting that maybe people shouldn't be form captains if they couldn't keep order. Jo dismissed it, crossly. Form captains shouldn't have to do prefects' jobs for them. Even Robbie would agree with that.

5

'Ready, Jo?'

Jo nodded. Elizabeth began her run-up, a loping jog trot, and bowled. Elizabeth's bowling was deceptive: it looked easy, until you came to play it. The ball had a nasty habit of suddenly zipping away at the last moment, taking the unwary batsman by surprise and spinning off the edge of the bat into the eagerly waiting hands of first slip or the wicket keeper – who, for the moment, for practice purposes, was Nadge.

Jo had been in the nets facing Elizabeth's bowling for almost ten minutes. She knew now what to expect. She braced herself, remembering Andy's words – 'Keep you *bat* over the *ball.*'

One, two, three, advance down the pitch to meet it, shoulders squared, DON'T TAKE YOUR EYE OFF IT, then *clonk*! The deeply satisfying sound of bat coming into contact with ball, sending it cracking out past cover and on towards the boundary – or where the boundary would have been had they been playing a real match.

Elizabeth threw up her arms in mock despair. Over her shoulder, to Wendy Armstrong, who had stopped to watch, she cried: 'This child is *hammering* me!' It was the third time Jo had dispatched her to the boundary. Of course she realized that Elizabeth wasn't bowling flat out, as she would to members of the first or second elevens, but all the same it wasn't everyone who could stand up to her even at half strength. Gerry, Matty, the Bookends, had all gone down like ninepins. Fij, who was stylish, had lasted three overs but without actually scoring any runs (what would have been runs). Nadge, who wasn't in the least stylish but had unerring ball sense, had hooked and slashed to great effect for the first five balls before having her middle stump knocked out by the sixth. Jo was the only one so far who had managed to survive – *and* hit some boundaries. Andy's tuition was paying off.

Elizabeth prepared to bowl again: Jo took up her stance. She was beginning to feel confident and to enjoy herself.

The ball flew down the pitch, Jo raised her bat.

'Howzat?' shrieked Nadge, from behind the wicket. She tossed the ball triumphantly in the air.

'Well caught!' cried Elizabeth. 'And about time, too . . . you were getting me worried!'

Jo grinned. She knew Elizabeth was only teasing: she *wanted* people to batter her bowling. She was looking for new blood for the Under-14s.

'Who's next?' said Elizabeth. 'Who have we got left?'

Barge and Bozzy were the only two remaining. Claire refused to play cricket because of her precious ankles (Claire was training to be a ballet dancer), Melanie thought all sports were a drag (and therefore so did Ash), the rest – Jool, Pru, Naomi, the Lollipop – were all worse than useless.

Jo watched, from cover point, as Barge swaggered to the crease. Barge played cricket as she did everything else, upfront and bellicose, heaving her bat like a sledgehammer. Wham! *Crack*. THUD! Clunk! BASH. Occasionally she connected, and the Mouse, standing precariously close at silly mid-off, squeaked with terror and ducked for her life; but more often than not she simply swiped at the air, and the ball went sailing through to Nadge, who was performing wonders of agility behind the wicket.

Barge lasted one and a half overs.

Bozzy then came in and was out first ball, caught by a surprised Mouse.

'Try again,' said Elizabeth, kindly, and tossed up another.

Obligingly Bozzy lifted her bat and spooned the ball straight back.

'One more?' said Elizabeth.

This time, Bozzy stepped backwards and sat on the stumps.

'Don't worry,' said Elizabeth, 'it's only your third week. We'll try you out on some bowling next time. But for the moment I'd like Nadia, Jo and Felicity to turn up for team practice on Tuesdays. The rest of you, keep at it! It's early days yet.'

'My cup runneth over,' exulted Fij, as she and Jo walked back to the cloakrooms together. 'Does your cup runneth over?'

'Positively *gushes*,' agreed Jo.

Being asked to turn up for team practice did not necessarily mean you were going to get a place on the team, but at least it meant you were being considered. She was already in the form rounders team, and along with Fij was reserve for the House Under-13s. (Nadge, needless to say, was in the House team.) Her loathsome Geography homework on the agricultural belts of the Mississippi had come back marked 'Excellent map!' which was practically unheard of, since Jo had no talent whatsoever for drawing – her maps usually looked as if a fly with a wooden leg had fallen into the inkpot and gone clumping across the page – Mrs Stanley had told her that if she continued to improve she might *just* pass her Maths exam, and at half term the school mag. was due out with Jo's poem that she had written last term, all about Fat Lollipop trying to slim.

> *I look in the mirror and what do I see?*
> *A shadow of the former me.*

Everyone was agreed that Jo's poem was going to be far and away the best in the mag.

'So much better than all this *drivel* that they print by the Sixth,' grumbled Barge.

'Kay Wyman actually wrote a poem last year in some kind of foreign langauge,' marvelled Bozzy.

'Greek,' said Fij. 'Actually.'

Bozzy tossed her plaits. 'Might just as well have been Outer Mongolian for all the sense it made!'

'Well, of course, it's just showing off,' agreed Barge. 'Nobody could understand it. She probably couldn't herself. She only did it to prove she's a genius. At least one thing I will say for Jammy is that she makes no attempt to write above her station – and when I say station,' she added, for the benefit of Bozzy's muddle brain, 'I do not refer to places such as King's Cross, you understand.'

'Or Euston,' said Fij, helpfully.

'Or Euston,' said Barge.

Bozzy nodded, sagely. 'What you are trying to say is that Jam is just as ordinarily averagely moronic as the rest of us.'

'Precisely. *Not* an intellectual giant, by any manner of means. But there you have it,' said Barge, who liked to wrap up her arguments (such as they were) in neat little parcels and tie them securely with bits of string. 'That, I fancy, is the secret.'

'Secret of what?' said Bozzy.

'Her success, you idiot!'

Jo was used, by now, to receiving these dubious sort of compliments from Barge and Bozzy. They meant well; and anyway Miss Lloyd had seen her poem and said, 'By the way, Jo, I must congratulate you! You made me laugh out loud.'

If it hadn't been for the dreadful responsibility of the blue badge, Jo could have been blissfully happy that summer term. If 1N hadn't taken it into their heads to behave so abominably she could still have been happy. They had never behaved like this with Gerry. With Jo in charge – or not in charge, as the case more often was – they simply ran riot.

When she made one of her admittedly not very convincing attempts at exercising control, they either jeered at her or told her to stop behaving like Mrs Thatcher.

One morning Miss Lloyd was away again and, instead of the Prole appearing in the classroom, Mrs Stanley introduced a new teacher to them.

'This is Miss Moston, who has come to look after you

for a few days while Miss Lloyd is away. As I think you know, Miss Lloyd's mother is not very well, in fact she is very seriously ill, so I want you to bear that in mind and moderate your behaviour accordingly.' Mrs Stanley's gaze raked the back row of the class as she said it. 'We all know the old adage: while the cat is away, the mice will play – which, put another way, simply means taking advantage of a situation. In this case, I have to say, it would be a very cheap and squalid advantage. I hope you can be trusted. Miss Moston, this is 1N. I leave them to you.'

Jo stared, along with everyone else. She had never seen a teacher quite like Miss Moston. Her face was big and round, with a wide stretchy mouth full of sticky-out teeth and a small blob of a nose on which were perched huge owly spectacles all colours of the rainbow. Her hair, which was bright yellow, hung in a shaggy mane over her eyes, so that she had to keep tossing her head to see through it.

A poor substitute for Miss Lloyd and her perfumed elegance. On the other hand, she certainly couldn't be called dowdy, like Mrs Denver in her shapeless washed-out woollies and baggy skirts. Miss Moston, in spite of being quite old, possibly even older than Jo's mum, was wearing trendy black leggings and trainers, with a long black jacket over the top and a CND badge in her lapel.

Promising, thought Jo. 'A fright,' said Barge, after-wards. Jo disagreed. She didn't think Miss Moston was a fright. *Weird*, perhaps; but definitely interesting.

'Now, people,' she said, as Mrs Stanley left the class (with a sharp look over her shoulder as she went), 'I am Marian Moston, *thus*,' and she took up a piece of chalk and wrote it on the board, *Marian Moston*, and then in brackets after: *(Ms)*.

'Note,' she said, tapping the *Ms*. 'I count myself a feminist. I take it for granted we are all feminists here. Being a feminist does not mean burning your brassieres –' a shocked titter ran round the room. One or two people, Jo included, actually blushed. A teacher, to be talking of brassieres! 'Nor does it mean doing you-know-what to men.'

Silence. Everyone would have liked to ask what you-know-what was, but nobody could quite pluck up the courage. They were, for the moment, stunned.

'It takes two of every species,' continued Ms Moston, supremely unaware (or so it seemed) of the consternation she was causing, 'to produce a third; so until such time as we can dispense with the other sex,' (Bozzy giggled, rather violently) 'by creating life in laboratories, it looks,' said Ms Moston, with a radiant smile, 'as if we are stuck with them. It behoves us, therefore, to make the best of a bad situation. We can only try to civilize. Let that be our aim, people: to civilize the cruder sex. I hope we are all in agreement?'

Ms Moston brandished a large toothy beam at those sitting in the front row. (The front row twitched, nervously.) Jo, safely tucked away in her corner next to Fij, felt her face split into an answering grin. She couldn't help it: Ms Moston's smile was infectious.

'That's right!' said Ms Moston. 'Someone's got the message.' (Matty swivelled in her desk to stare accusingly at Jo.) 'No! Being feminist, my dears, basically means fulfilling our potential as individuals. We must not let ourselves be straitjacketed! Have babies, by all means –' Bozzy tittered, and hastily changed it to a hiccup – 'get married if you must, but AVOID THE DREADED STRAITJACKET. Now! You know who I am, let me find out who you are.'

By the end of the day, when most of the Upper School had come into contact with Ms Moston one way or another, the word was out that 'the new supply teacher is a nutter'.

'But she is quite nice,' said Jo, anxiously, to Matty, on the way home.

'Well, if you like that kind of thing,' said Matty. She sniffed. 'Telling people to go and have babies without getting married.'

'I don't think she quite meant that,' said Jo, blushing. (She did *wish* she could stop turning beetroot whenever people mentioned words like babies or brassieres.) 'But in any case,' she added, 'lots of people do.'

'Better not let your mum hear you talk that way,' said Matty.

'I'm not saying it's a good thing, necessarily,' said Jo. 'I was just saying that people *do*.'

'Doesn't make it right, does it?'

'I didn't say it made it right.'

'No, and you didn't say it made it wrong. Nor did she. You can tell where *she* stands, ugly old bag.'

'I don't think people ought to be unkind to her,' said Jo. 'She's only trying to teach us how to make the most of ourselves and not be stopped from doing things just because we're girls.'

'Yeah, like sumo wrestling,' said Matty. 'I've always wanted to take up sumo wrestling.'

When Matty decided she didn't like someone there

55

was no arguing her out of it. Jo knew from experience that it only made her more stubborn.

'Well, anyway,' she said, 'it was a good idea about the essay, wasn't it?'

Ms Moston had asked them to write 'just a few short paragraphs' on one of their favourite literary heroines and the book that she came from.

'Don't you think?' said Jo.

'Yeah, smashing,' said Matty. 'Think I'll choose Noddy.'

There was a short silence, then Jo said: 'Noddy's not a heroine.'

'So what?' said Matty.

Next day, in English, when Ms Moston collected their homework, she said, 'Let us just have a quick run round and – Nadia!' She broke off in astonishment as Nadge suddenly shot out of her desk and set off at a jog along the gangway. 'My dear girl! Whatever is the matter?'

'We're not girls, we're women!' shouted the Mouse.

'If she's a woman she must be a bleeding midget,' said Matty.

'Girls! People! No squabbling. Remember we are sisters. Nadia –' With an energetic sweep, Ms Moston caught up with Nadge and brought her to a halt. 'Do stop jigging about, dear. I know you're games captain, but this is an English lesson not a rehearsal for the Olympic Games.'

Nadge looked at her, reproachfully. 'You said we were to have a quick run round.'

'Yes. I did; that is perfectly true. But we don't want to take things *too* literally, do we? Go and collect the homework for me and let's see who you've all chosen as

56

your heroines: I am very excited by this! Joanne? Who have you chosen?'

Jo had taken the project very seriously. She had spent almost an hour going through her books and trying to decide on a favourite heroine. In the end she had settled for Sarah Crewe from *A Little Princess*.

'Ah, yes!' Ms Moston gave one of her toothy beams. 'Not a feminist, of course, but always a favourite. Felicity?'

Fij had chosen Jo from *Little Women*. ('Now Jo *was* a feminist, of sorts,' Ms Moston agreed. But Jo had married boring old Professor Baer. That had ruined her in modern Jo's eyes.)

'Chloë?' said Ms Moston. 'Isn't this fun? I am enjoying myself! Who has Chloë chosen?'

Bozzy, with a perfectly straight face, said: 'I've chosen Anne, from *Five Go Adventuring Again*.'

Anne? Jo looked at her, incredulously. Anne was one of the most helpless, useless, idiotic creatures ever written about. And anyway, Bozzy had surely grown out of Enid Blyton?

Ms Moston blinked, but refrained from comment and wrote it on the board along with Sarah Crewe and Jo March.

'Margery?' she said.

Barge stood up, solid and foursquare, behind her desk. 'Anne from *Five Go Down to the Sea Again*,' she said.

Emma and the Mouse had also chosen Anne (*Five On A Treasure island*, *Five Go to Smuggler's Top*). They must have arranged it together, as some kind of stupid joke. Jo felt ashamed of them. It wasn't funny. It was just childish. Even Matty, in the end, had come up with

57

something sensible. She had chosen Alice, from *Alice's Adventures in Wonderland*. (Ms Moston said, '*That's* an interesting choice,' and Jo instantly wished that she had chosen it, especially as Matty subsequently confessed that she thought *Alice* was a 'really dumb kind of book' and she'd only picked on it because it was the first thing that came to mind.)

In the playground at break Fij rounded indignantly on Barge and Bozzy.

'Why didn't you tell me what you were going to do? We could all have done it!'

'We didn't tell you,' said Bozzy, ''cause you'd have told Jam and she'd have been all prissy and disapproving.'

'Yes.' Barge looked severely at Jo. 'You are showing alarming tendencies that way.'

Jo flushed, but felt moved to protest. 'I don't mind a joke but that was just silly.'

'You may think it so,' said Barge, loftily. 'Those of us who appreciate a bit of intellectual clowning found it highly amusing.'

'Anne!' said Bozzy. She sniggered.

'You might at least have chosen George,' said Jo. 'She at least was some kind of heroine.'

'It wouldn't have been funny then, would it?' said Bozzy.

'I don't think it's funny anyway,' said Jo.

'Oh, shut up!' Barge turned away. 'You're losing *all* your sense of humour.'

The behaviour of 1N, during that week of Miss Lloyd's absence, lurched from bad to worse. In Private Study Barge and Bozzy now played consequences quite openly. Nadge plugged in to her personal stereo and danced in the gangway – 'She can't help it!' they chorused at the Prole. 'She's got this thing where she can't keep still' – the Bookends developed an irritating habit of asking questions in unison, like a double act – 'Please, Proline, may we be excused?' 'Please, Proline, may we look at the dictionary?' – Fat Lollipop nonchalantly passed round slices of pizza (made by her Italian dad, who ran his own restaurant), Jool and Matty conducted whispered conversations under their desk lids. The Prole, like Jo, seemed to have given up all attempt at keeping order.

If they didn't misbehave quite so blatantly with Ms Moston it was because she was still largely an unknown quantity. How far could she be pushed before she turned nasty? 1N didn't know but were doing their best to find out. Ostentatiously, they addressed her as Ms (pronounced Mzz).

'Mzz! Mzz! Ask me, Mzz!' pleaded Jool, waving her arms about.

'No, Mzz! Don't ask her, Mzz! Ask me, Mzz!'

'Mzz! Mzz! What about me, Mzz?'

Soon the whole room was alive with the sound of buzzing.

'Do you think there's a wasps' nest in here, Mzz?' asked Matty.

'No,' said Ms Moston. 'I think you are enjoying yourselves. Well, that's all right! You enjoy yourselves. Don't get locked into any straitjackets, that's all I ask.'

'Mzz!' Now it was Nadge waving her hand in the air. 'Mzz, you know when you said about not doing you-know-what to men, Mzz. What did you mean, Mzz?'

'I meant we must not do to men what we do to male cats and dogs to keep them from straying.'

Pause, while the class digested this.

'We never did it to our dog, Mzz!'

'Why can't we do it to men, Mzz?'

'Because that is no way to deal with the problem. Let civilization be our watchword!'

'Mzz!' Now it was Matty's turn. 'You know that other thing you said? About having babies? And then you said about getting married. Well, shouldn't it be the other way round, Mzz? Shouldn't people get married first and have babies afterwards?'

'Yeah, that's what we've always been taught, Mzz!'

'My mum wouldn't like it, if she knew you was telling us to go and have babies without being married.'

'My mum'd go spare.'

'Yeah, and mine!'

'Have you ever had a baby, Mzz?'

'Mzz can't, she's not married!'

'Doesn't make any difference, Mzz said so.'

'Mzz said you got to have two of everything to make a third.'

'Two pencils –'

'Two rulers –'

'Two rubbers –'

'How they s'pposed to do it, Mzz?'

'If my pencil married your rubber –'

'Can't have a pencil marrying a *rubber*.'

'All right. If my pencil married your pencil –'

'They'd have a little crayon!'

Oh, hilarity! 1N were having the time of their lives. But there was going to be trouble, thought Jo, if Miss Lloyd or Mrs Stanley came to hear of it.

'You mustn't get all boring about it, you know,' said Fij, kindly, when Jo one lunch break confided her worries. 'We only voted for you as a joke. No one expects you to *do* anything.'

'No, I know that,' said Jo, 'but what about the Cup?'

'Well, yes. The Cup is important, but let's face it,' said Fij, cheerfully, 'we've never been noted for our good behaviour. Not even when the Dictator was in charge. We've always had a *reputation*. And anyway, we're bound to win the interhouse rounders and the cricket and everything. Nellie's always does, so a few odd order marks here and there aren't going to make much difference. You really must stop huffing and puffing and making yourself unhappy. Otherwise,' said Fij, 'I shall begin to wish I hadn't voted for you.'

'I sometimes wish you hadn't,' said Jo.

6

'You got this prefect called Chlorine, or something?' said Tom, one Saturday morning to Jo, over breakfast.

'*Chlorine*?'

'Well, or something like that. Some stupid name.'

'You mean Proline,' said Jo.

'Yeah; Proline.'

'Why? What about her?'

'Nadge was telling me, last night at the Club.' Tom had a soft spot for Nadge (one of the few girls he didn't think soppy) and Nadge, for some reason Jo could never understand, seemed to think that Tom was not absolutely and utterly obnoxious.

'What was she telling you?'

'About this brill idea she's got.'

Jo frowned, concentrating her attention on her cereal until Mrs Jameson, pottering about at the washing machine, had gone into the back garden with a load of damp washing.

'What brill idea?'

'Brill idea for having fun.'

'What sort of fun?'

'Ho, ho,' said Tom, 'wouldn't you like to know?'

Jo flipped a Rice Krispie at him. 'Tell me!'

'Can't.' Tom shook his head. 'It's a secret.'

'Who said?'

'Nadge did.'

'So what's she telling you for?'

''Cause she wanted to know what I thought of it and whether we'd ever done anything like it.'

Like what? wondered Jo; but she kept her head bent over her Rice Krispies. She wasn't going to give him the satisfaction of knowing that she cared. He was only doing it to niggle her.

'It's a great idea,' said Tom. 'I think we might try it out on one of ours.'

'One of your what?'

'Prefects. Bodger Dodworth; *he's* a prat.'

Jo knew all about poor Bodger Dodworth, whose real name was Rodger. Boys like Tom played horrible tricks on him. Last term they had shut him in the games cupboard; she hoped Nadge wasn't going to try anything like that with Proline.

Jo, of late, had started to feel sorry for the Prole. She knew she was useless, and she still hadn't forgiven her for being petty and accusing Jo of cheating when all she'd been doing was trying to stop people making fun of her, but last time they had had Private Study the Bookends had done one of their celebrated double acts – ''Scuse me, Prole!' ''Scuse her, Prole.' 'May I ask a question, Prole?' 'May she ask a question, Prole?' – which had reduced the whole class to giggles and Proline to a blushing heap. Jo knew what it was like to blush.

'I hope it's nothing nasty,' she said.

'It's not nasty, it's fun. And I can't tell you what it is, so it's no good nagging at me. You'll just have to wait and see. If I told you what it was you'd go and put the mockers on it.'

63

'What mockers?' Jo spoke through a mouthful of Rice Krispies. 'What's mockers?'

'Means you'd squash it,' said Tom. ''Cause you're a killjoy.'

'I'm not a killjoy!'

'Yes, you are; Matty said so. She said you'd become a right bossy bit and a miserable killjoy.'

'Matty did?' That hurt. Matty was supposed to be her friend.

'Ever since you got to be form captain and started needling people. Always going on about *order* marks and *house* points.'

Jo flushed. 'Well, it's their fault for voting for me. *I* didn't want to be voted for. It's horrid being form captain, it makes everybody hate you.'

'It wouldn't if you didn't boss people.'

'I don't boss them!'

'Matty says you do. She says you've even started bossing them in the canteen.'

'That was because they were flicking bits of food around!'

Nadge and Lee Powell, that had been, having a flicking match with Matty and Jool. Jo had only been trying to stop them before Mrs Stanley caught them at it and gave them order marks. Matty had told her to bug off and Lee Powell had told her to drop dead. (And Mrs Stanley had *still* given them order marks.)

'You've got a nerve,' said Tom, 'having a go at people for flicking food around.' He looked down at his T-shirt where the Rice Krispie had landed. 'You ought to practise what you preach,' said Tom.

'It's different at home! I wouldn't do it at *school*.'

'That's double standards, that is. And what about this nutty teacher that goes on about babies?'

'Ms Moston. What about her?'

'Matty says you keep on at them about her, as well.'

'Yes, because they're hateful to her! I know she's nutty but she can't help it, and at least she isn't mean.'

'People that are nutty shouldn't be teaching.'

'Prob'ly *makes* them nutty, having to teach yobs like you!'

'That's right,' said Tom. 'Now she's having a go at me. Ning ning ning!' He made snapping motions at her with his fingers. 'You're getting to be a right pain, you are.'

'Well, but it's not fair!' cried Jo. 'I didn't ask to be form captain!'

'So resign,' said Tom.

Jo fell silent, brooding into her cereal bowl.

'If you go on being it,' said Tom, 'that shows that secretly inside yourself you *like* being it and you *like* bossing people around. If you didn't like being it you'd stop being it.'

Tom made it sound so simple. But it wasn't! Jo had discussed it with Robbie. She had said to him, 'Do you actually like being head of form?' and Robbie had thought about it, rubbing a finger up and down his nose as he did so, and finally said that sometimes he did and sometimes he didn't, but what he mainly felt was that it was a responsibility that had been put on him and it would be cowardly to back out of it.

That was a bit how Jo felt. She kept remembering Miss Lloyd saying that she expected good things of her. To resign would be admitting defeat, and no one liked to do that.

Tom shrugged. 'It's up to you,' he said. 'But just don't moan about it.'

'I'm not moaning,' muttered Jo; but she still didn't think that it was fair.

Over the weekend she played cricket in the park with Tom and Robbie, and Matty and Miles, who was Matty's brother and was in the same form as Tom and Robbie. On Sunday she went to watch Andy and her dad playing for the local cricket team, known as the Petersham Peregrines. She was there all day, from the first over to the last, and was allowed to help with the scoreboard and sell match cards. She forgot all about Nadge's brilliant idea for baiting Proline; it wasn't until Wednesday, when she looked at her timetable and saw that the first period after lunch was Private Study, that Tom's words came back to her.

Urgently she sought out Fij, who was down in the cloakroom picking a scab off her knee. Fortunately Barge and Bozzy were not around. She wasn't sure she would have been brave enough to say anything in front of Barge and Bozzy; they had been a bit hostile just lately.

'What's Nadge planning to do in Private Study?' she said.

Fij jumped, guiltily. 'How did you know she was planning anything?'

''Cause Tom told me – but he wouldn't tell me what.'

'No. Well!' Fij gave a little laugh. It didn't quite sound convincing. 'It's probably better if you don't know.'

'Why? It isn't something beastly?'

'It isn't in the *least* bit beastly. Honest! It's just going to be fun.'

66

'So why can't I know?'

'Because you'd only start worrying,' said Fij, 'and wittering on about order marks. Admit it! You would!'

Jo looked at her, reproachfully. 'We're supposed to be a gang,' she said. 'We're not supposed to have secrets.'

'No, I know. But –' Fij blotted at her knee, now satisfactorily denuded of scab and oozing blood. 'The fact is,' she said, awkwardly, 'Nadge made us promise not to. But it's only a bit of *fun*!'

'So when's it going to happen?' said Jo. 'Today?'

Fij's gaze shifted, evasively. 'That's up to Nadge to decide. Maybe it won't happen at all. It isn't actually definite,' she said. 'You don't want to get yourself into a state about it.'

'I'm not getting into a state,' said Jo.

'That's good. I thought you were.'

'Well, I'm not.'

'It would be silly, really, over such a very *minor* thing. I mean,' said Fij, 'let's face it . . . it's only the Prole. If it were Mrs Stanley, or – or Elizabeth or someone – well! I could understand you might be a bit uptight. But the *Prole* –'

'I don't wish to know about it,' said Jo, grandly. 'I wash my hands of the whole affair.'

It was what her mother always said when she rebelled at taking responsibility for something that 'one of you ruddy rotten brats' (usually Tom) insisted on doing in spite of repeatedly being asked not to. Jo had repeatedly – well, on at least two occasions – beseeched the class to 'think of the Cup'. If they wouldn't listen to reason, then that was their problem; she wanted nothing more to do with it. All the same, it would be a relief if they behaved themselves for once.

For the first thirty minutes of the forty-minute period 1N's behaviour was impeccable. Jo relaxed, and so did the Prole. Jo at any rate should have known better: after all, she had been warned. Yet when it started it took her every bit as unawares as it did the Prole. In fact, she didn't immediately realize that anything *had* started. All she knew was that one minute she was wrestling with her Maths homework, the next she was almost startled out of her skin by the sound of Nadge sneezing. Nadge didn't just sneeze an ordinary sneeze, she sneezed a sneeze that echoed right round the classroom, bouncing off the walls and causing the very windows to shake in their frames.

'Aaaaaaaaaaaaaaaaa-TISH-ooooooooooooooooooooo ooooo!' went Nadge's sneeze.

Jo's hand shot involuntarily across the page. Fij stifled a giggle. The Prole, made cross through sheer fright, snapped, 'Can't you sneeze quietly, Nadia?'

'I cahd helb id,' said Nadge, clamping a large white handkerchief to her nose. 'I thig I god a subber gowd.'

'Pardon?' said the Prole.

'Summer cold!' yelled the class.

'Or hay fever,' added Barge.

'Or hay peber,' agreed Nadge.

'Well, in future try putting your hand in front of your mouth.'

For perhaps a minute there was silence. And then Nadge sneezed again – 'Ah-TISH-ooo!' It wasn't quite as long or as loud as before, but this time someone else sneezed, as well.

Jo looked up quickly, and saw that Barge now had a

large white handkerchief pressed to her nose. Her heart sank. So this was Nadge's brill idea! It was a variant of the book-dropping scam. She wondered if the Prole had tumbled to it yet, but it seemed not, for apart from a brief glance of annoyance in Barge's direction and an irritably muttered, 'Do you have to be so uncouth?' she made no comment.

Jo dug Fij in the ribs: Fij, in response, wrote *FUN*, heavily underlined, on a page of her rough book. Jo supposed that it probably would have been fun, had she not been burdened with thoughts of Elizabeth, and Miss Lloyd, and the Cup, and the fearsome responsibility of the blue badge. After all, it wasn't really doing any harm.

'Ah-TISH-ooooo!' screamed Nadge, Barge, Bozzy and Fij in unison.

'Ah-TISH-ooooo!' screamed Nadge, Barge, Bozzy, Fij and the Bookends.

'Ah-TISH-ooooo!' screamed Nadge, Barge, Bozzy, Fij, the Bookends, Matty, Jool and Claire.

'Ah-TISH-ooooo!' screamed Nadge, Barge, Bozzy, etc., plus Melanie, Ash and the Lollipop.

'Ah-TISH-ooooo!' finally screamed everyone all together, with the sole exception of Jo.

Jo couldn't believe it: even Gerry & Co. were joining in. It was as if Gerry were saying, '*I*'m not form captain, it's not up to me to set a good example.' And where Gerry led, Pru and Naomi automatically followed. They sat there, the three of them, whooping and sneezing into their large white handkerchiefs the same as everyone else. The sound of fifteen people performing orchestrated sneezes had to be heard to be believed. Jo was only surprised the windows didn't break.

The Prole, tight-lipped and white-faced, stood at the front of the room with her hands pressed to her ears. It seemed to be a gesture of despair rather than an attempt to blot out the noise.

Fij turned to look at Jo, her eyes dancing over the top of her handkerchief. (Where had they all got large white handkerchieves *from*? Their fathers' handkerchief drawers?)

'Aaaaaaaa-TISH-oooooooooo!' went Fij, rather pointedly, at Jo.

If Gerry could do it . . . Jo dug her hand into her pocket. She didn't have a large white handkerchief but a small blue one would do just as well.

'Aaaaaaaa –' began Jo.

She never got as far as 'tishoo': the door was flung open and Mrs Stanley came stalking in. Mrs Stanley was definitely not a person to be trifled with. The sneezing stopped abruptly, some people in the middle of a *tish*, some at the end of an *oo*.

'What, may I ask, is going on in here?' said Mrs Stanley.

The Prole took her hands from her ears and spread them before her in a gesture of helplessness. Only Nadge was cheeky enough to attempt a reply: 'We've all got hay fever 'cause of the weather.'

'Oh! Have you? Well, in that case you can all sign the order mark book. That should get rid of it.'

A slight muffled gasp ran round the class. Sixteen order marks all in one go! It was Fij, bravely, who put up her hand.

'Yes, Felicity. What do you want?'

'Jammy wasn't doing it,' said Fij. 'That is, I mean, Jo.'

'Very well, then! The rest of you can sign the order mark book, and you, Nadia, can sign twice. I don't doubt you were at the bottom of things, as usual.'

'I had a tiggle in by doze,' said Nadge.

'Be very careful,' said Mrs Stanley. 'I am capable of great wrath.' Her gaze roamed the class. 'I'm surprised at you, Geraldine. I should have thought, as form captain, you would have known better.'

Gerry's cheeks were brick red. Pru, somewhat spitefully, said, 'It's not Gerry, it's her.'

Everyone, including Mrs Stanley, turned to look at Jo.

'Joanne Jameson!' said Mrs Stanley. 'Well!'

'Joanne Jameson!' mimicked Melanie, as they collected up their books for the next class. 'Well!'

Within seconds, the cry had been taken up: 'Joanne Jameson!' chorused the Bookends.

'Joanne Jameson!' echoed Barge and Bozzy.

'Joanne Jameson! *Well*!'

'Don't worry,' whispered Fij to Jo. 'At least she knows you weren't joining in.'

It was small comfort, thought Jo, when set against sixteen order marks.

7

'I suppose you thought it was amusing?' said Miss Lloyd.

Her voice was ice-cold, her blue eyes snapped. 1N writhed uncomfortably in their desks.

'I have just one word to describe you,' said Miss Lloyd. 'That word is contemptible.' Her lip curled: her scorn was withering. 'You are bullies. And like all bullies, you are cowards. You're not brave enough to try that sort of thing on with me, so you wait till my back is turned and pick on the weakest links you can find – a teacher who is new to the school, and a prefect who is still trying to find her feet. Despicable! Utterly despicable!'

1N cringed and did their best to slump down out of sight behind the person in front. Those who didn't have anyone in front – Claire, Nadge, Naomi, the Lollipop – kept their heads bent over their desk lids.

'Typical bully behaviour,' said Miss Lloyd. 'You deserve to be thoroughly ashamed of yourselves! Every single one of you.'

Jo didn't know whether she was included in 'every single one' or not. It really wouldn't be fair, because after all *she* hadn't joined in, and furthermore, back at the beginning, she had done her best to put a stop to all the bullying (and had been accused of cheating for her pains). Jo sat stiff and straight in her desk, in an attempt to cut herself off from the rest of the class.

'I shall expect you all to write a suitable letter of apology for that final disgraceful incident. You can hand them in tomorrow morning, and please note, NO EXCUSES WILL BE ACCEPTED. I don't want to hear any stories –' Miss Lloyd looked directly at Nadge as she spoke – 'of the baby being sick over it or the dog chewing it up. I want those letters here first thing in the morning. From everybody.'

Does that mean me? wondered Jo.

'Furthermore, when I say letter,' said Miss Lloyd, 'I mean letter. I do not mean a one-line note. Do I make myself plain?'

The class nodded, solemnly. Not even Nadge dared defy Miss Lloyd.

'Very well,' said Miss Lloyd. 'You may now go to your break. Jo, I'd like you to stay behind a moment, please.'

Fij pulled a commiserating face from under cover of her desk lid as she put her English books away, but Jo wasn't too worried. Miss Lloyd had obviously heard from Mrs Stanley that the one person who wasn't playing up was Jo Jameson. It was a relief to know that she knew about it without having to be told – because how could you put your own hand up and say 'Please, it wasn't me: *I* wasn't doing it'? Jo was glad, all the same, that Miss Lloyd hadn't drawn attention to it in front of the others; it would have made her seem so goody-goody.

'Well, Jo!' Miss Lloyd stood, looking down at her. It seemed to Jo that there was more than a hint of reproach in her voice. But why, when Jo hadn't done anything? 'What am I to say to you?' said Miss Lloyd.

Jo wrinkled her forehead, under her fringe.

'I did warn you that being form captain wasn't easy. Are you finding the task too much for you?'

Jo felt a redness creep into her cheeks.

'If you are,' said Miss Lloyd, 'just say so and I'm sure Gerry will be only too happy to take over.'

Was Miss Lloyd throwing down a challenge? Or was she inviting Jo to resign? Jo rubbed her wrinkled forehead with a finger, trying to decide.

'I know,' said Miss Lloyd, 'that you weren't actually involved in last Wednesday's appalling behaviour – yes, and Gerry was, I'm aware of that also – but I can't help feeling that had you managed to instil a proper sense of responsibility into the class at the beginning, they wouldn't have disgraced themselves. They're not a bad bunch, but they do need a firm hand.' Like Gerry's. But everyone was just about *sick* of Gerry. 'If you don't feel capable of wielding that firm hand –'

Miss Lloyd paused, to monitor Jo's response.

'I'll try a bit harder,' said Jo.

Really, it was all she *could* say. What kind of person would limply admit to failure?

'I hope that you will,' said Miss Lloyd. 'I still have faith in you. I shouldn't like to think it was misplaced.'

Jo heaved a sigh.

'Believe me,' said Miss Lloyd, 'nobody likes having to be a martinet. But if you can earn people's respect you've won at least half the battle. You don't earn respect by throwing your weight around, but neither do you earn it by just sitting back and doing nothing. At the moment they're having a ball – let's face it! They are, aren't they? They're behaving like little children suddenly let out of the nursery – and they think you're a

74

pushover. But sooner or later there's got to be one person, just one person, who rounds them up and gets them organized and pointed in the right direction. That person is you.'

Jo nodded.

'Of course there'll be some resistance, they're going to resent it just to begin with, but once they realize you mean business you'll find they follow you. But you do have to exert yourself, and you do have to be prepared for a certain amount of hostility. Do you think you can face it?'

'I'll do my best,' said Jo.

'That's all I ask of you: that you do your best. I don't feel, so far, that you have. I shall hope from now on to see some improvement. I'm not looking for miracles, I don't expect you to turn Nadia into a plaster saint overnight. But just do the best you can. Oh, and Jo! Instead of writing a letter of apology to Pauline, I suggest you write her a letter of support. I think she would appreciate that. Yes?'

Miss Lloyd nodded, briskly, and swept on her way. Jo's mouth fell open. She stood, foolishly, arms gangling at her sides. *Pauline*? Trust Bozzy to go and get it wrong!

Outside in the playground a little knot of Nellie First Years – Barge, Bozzy, Fij, the Bookends – were giggling themselves into fits rehearsing their letters of apology.

'Dear Proline, We are sorry we frightened you by our loud sneezing –'

'Loud and un*couth* sneezing.'

'Loud and un*couth* sneezing. Next time we have hay fever we will try to have it more quietly.'

'And not alarm you with our explosions.'

'And not alarm you with our explosions. Alternatively, we could bring you some earplugs to put in your ears –'

'And a mask to put over your face so you will not catch the horrid germs.'

'And to hide your horrid face.'

Shriek. Hoot. Mirth.

'Oh, dear!' gasped Barge. 'I shall die laughing!'

Fij turned to Jo, who was hovering on the outskirts. 'We're planning our apology letters to Proline.'

'It's Pauline,' said Jo, 'actually.' But nobody heard her.

On her way back into school at the end of break she found Gerry waiting solicitously at the entrance.

'So how did it go?' said Gerry, trying to sound casual and at the same time oozing false concern from every pore.

'How did what go?' said Jo. (Pretend ignorance. Always the best policy.)

'Your little tête-à-tête with Miss Lloyd.'

'Oh! that.' Jo gave a careless snicker. Gerry was so *obvious*. 'I thought you were asking after my brain transplant.'

'Goodness me!' said Gerry, knitting her brow into a frown of deepest sympathy. 'So you've had one of those as well? You poor thing! I do hope Miss Lloyd wasn't *too* hard on you.'

If you mean, thought Jo, did she threaten to take my badge away and give it to you, the answer is no. Miss Lloyd had made it plain that she wanted Jo to carry on.

'Miss Lloyd and I,' said Jo, in tones that even Barge at her loftiest might have been envious of, 'have reached an understanding.'

76

'Oh, yes,' said Gerry, interested.

'While the rest of you write letters of apology, I am going to write a letter of support. Obviously,' said Jo, 'as I did nothing wrong I have nothing to apologize for.'

'No. Well, of course –' Gerry attempted a laugh of her own, but couldn't quite bring it off. 'Personally I shall offer Proline my deepest condolences.'

Whatever they are, thought Jo. 'It's Pauline,' she said, 'actually.' But Gerry had already gone scudding off to join Pru and Naomi and didn't hear her.

The form room, when they got back to it, was looking its usual shambles. After earlier rebuffs from Matty, and jeers from everyone else, Jo had more or less given up on it. Now she said to Matty, '*Could* you do something about cleaning up the mess? And look, whoever is flower monitor? These pot plants need water.'

'I'm not flower monitor,' said Matty.

'I know you're not.' Jo did her best to speak patiently and not show irritation. 'I never said you were, did I?'

'Don't you get on my case,' said Matty.

'Just stop bossing people,' said Barge. 'You're getting as bad as you-know-who.'

'Well, but who *is* flower monitor?' insisted Jo.

'I am,' said Melanie. 'And for your information those sort of pot plants don't need water. There are those that do and those that don't; and those are the sort that don't.'

'So why are they all brown and gungy, with half the leaves falling off?'

'They wouldn't be falling off if you hadn't just gone and plucked at them. Any leaves,' said Melanie, aggrieved, 'will come off if people with great fat hands go pulling at them.'

'And I s'ppose any plants will go brown if people with great fat eyes go looking at them?' retorted Jo. (She *hadn't* got fat hands. They were a perfectly ordinary sort of hands.) 'You're nothing better than a murderer,' said Jo. 'Plants do have feelings, you know.'

'Oh! She'll be wanting me to *talk* to them next.' Melanie advanced, dramatically, upon the wilting plants. 'There, my little diddy darlings! Diddums nasty bossy lady come and pullums ickle leafies off? Mummy kiss oo, make oo better . . . *mwa*!' said Melanie, bestowing her lips rather too enthusiastically upon a begonia, which promptly collapsed under the strain.

'It does look a little bit dry,' said Fij.

'It's not just dry, it's *parched*.' Jo dug a finger indignantly into the crumbling earth. 'That's criminal neglect, that is. If that were a dog you'd get done for it.'

'Dog!' Melanie tittered. 'She'll be confusing it with a chimpanzee next.'

Jo flushed, angrily. 'How d'you expect to get any House points for a windowful of dead things?'

Melanie huffed and puffed but finally, with a display of exaggerated impatience, went flouncing from the room to fetch a jug of water. Matty, meanwhile, grudgingly and with much grumbling, picked up the wastepaper basket and began trawling up the aisles, collecting rubbish.

'Dunno what schools employ caretakers for. I'm s'pposed to be coming here to learn things, not clear up other people's messes after them. I can clear up enough mess at home without coming here to do it . . . ugh! Orange peel! That's dis*gu*sting!'

'Well, don't blame me,' said Jo. 'People shouldn't be

eating oranges in the classroom. It's against the rules.'

'Oh, shut up about the rules!' said Barge.

'It's all very well saying shut up –'

'Shut up, shut up! You're like a mouth on a stick.'

'Yes, you are,' said Bozzy. 'You're like a horrible malicious glove puppet . . . always mouthing and carrying on.'

'As bad as Mrs Thatcher.'

'Don't do this, don't do that –'

'Accusing people of murder,' said Melanie, coming back with the water. 'You could get taken to court for that.'

'Yes, and you could get taken there for murder!' snapped Jo.

Melanie screeched, 'That's libel, that is!'

'Or slander,' said Gerry.

'Not if it's true,' said Jo. 'Which it is,' she added. 'That plant's never going to recover, and neither's any of the others, probably. We'll just end up with a windowful of corpses.'

'Oh, heavens! There she goes *again*,' said Barge.

'Let's ignore it,' said Bozzy. 'It's getting on my nerves.'

The plants were watered, the classroom was clean and tidy; they *would* do what she told them if she nagged at them long enough. But now they were mad at her and wouldn't talk. Even Fij was disapproving. It was all right Miss Lloyd saying 'be prepared for a certain amount of hostility', but Jo wasn't used to being unpopular.

During the lunch break, after they had eaten lunch together in the canteen (with Barge and Bozzy still doing their best to pretend that Jo wasn't there), Fij went off to

79

play in a tennis match while Barge and Bozzy linked up with the Bookends for another giggling session. So entranced had they been by their own sparkling wit and repartee, they were going to write a whole series of 'Dear Proline' letters and offer them for publication in next year's school mag. (if not indeed in *Private Eye*). They made it clear, without actually saying so, that Jo was not invited.

Jo mooched for a while, unhappily, about the playground. Matty and Jool were huddled in a corner with Dell Rivers and Susie Fern, two other black girls in the first year. They were all members of the Black Power Gang, which Lee Powell had founded last term. Matty had never seemed to care about being black when she and Jo were at Juniors; now she was becoming all strident and political. She wouldn't thank Jo for going and butting in even if Jo hadn't upset her by asking her to do her duties as tidiness monitor.

Gerry & Co. were feebly batting a tennis ball about, Melanie and Ash, with the Lollipop in attendance, were attempting to sunbathe in a small patch of watery sunshine, Claire was nowhere to be seen but was probably down in the cloakroom (where she had no right to be) practising her ballet. She would get an order mark if anyone found her, which someone was bound to do, sooner or later. It was a wonder she had got away with it for as long as she had. Jo decided, for want of anything better to do – and because she *was* form captain, even if it was a joke – to go down to the cloakroom and tell Claire to stop it.

Sure enough, she found Claire doing leg exercises in amongst the clothes pegs, using the window ledge as a *barre*.

'Why aren't you outside?' said Jo, watching in fascination, despite herself, as one of Claire's legs slowly unfolded at right angles to her body.

'Because I'm down here,' said Claire.

'I can see you're down here. What I want to know is *why* are you down here?'

'Because I'm doing my *battements*,' said Claire, pronouncing it '*battermon*' on account of it being French.

'You ought to do them in the playground,' said Jo. 'You're not supposed to stay in during the lunch break.'

'I always do them down here,' said Claire, changing sides and unfolding her other leg. With one slim hand clasped beneath her instep she casually extended her foot until it was on a level with her head. (Jo had tried and *tried* to do that. 'Standing on one foot like a mentally deficient stalk,' grumbled Bozzy. But you had to admit, thought Jo, it was impressive.) 'I've been doing it all term,' said Claire. 'Nobody's ever said anything.'

'That's only because they haven't caught you. If anyone catches you they'll give you an order mark.'

Claire lowered her leg back to the ground.

'You'd better move a bit,' she said. 'You'll get kicked standing there like that.'

What could you do? You couldn't *force* people to obey.

Jo left the cloakroom and trailed back up the steps to the playground. On the way she passed the green baize noticeboards, one for every House, where notices of meetings, drama rehearsals, games practices, etc., were pinned up. Also pinned up were the weekly contributions made by each form to the House total of

81

bonus points and order marks. All the houses had their own methods of charting progress. Nellie's favoured graphs – red for bonus points, green for order marks. Glancing casually as she passed, Jo was horrified to observe that the order mark graph for last week had a huge green curve climbing dizzily up the page on the right hand side. She moved closer, just to check. It could be the Second Years. In fact, it probably was. The First Years were probably squashed down next to them, so small they could hardly be seen.

It wasn't the Second Years. The graph made it only too horribly plain:

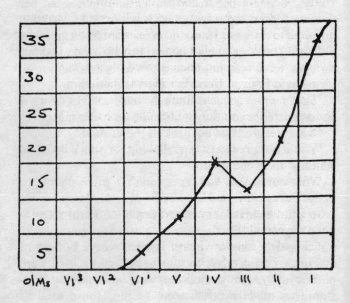

The First Years had acquired so many order marks during the course of the previous week that they very nearly went right off the page. . . .

Over *thirty*. That meant an average of – Jo was still trying to work it out (an average of *two and a bit per person*) when Elizabeth appeared.

'Greetings! Why so glum?' She leaned across Jo to pin a list of net practices on the board. 'You didn't expect to make the Firxt XI straight away, did you?'

Jo looked up at her, frowning. Elizabeth tapped a finger on a notice which Jo hadn't seen. It was the Under-14 cricket XI for next week's match against York – and Jo was down as 12th man! She had even been chosen above Nadge, who was a mere reserve along with Fij.

'Don't tell me you hadn't seen it?' teased Elizabeth. Jo, shyly, shook her head. 'So what was all the gloom in aid of? You looked like someone who's just taken a swipe at a full toss and been bowled for a duck!'

'I was looking at the order marks,' said Jo.

'Ye-e-e-e-s. . . .' Elizabeth cast an eye briefly upon the graph. 'They're not too healthy, are they?'

'It's my fault,' said Jo.

'What! You mean they all belong to you? That must be something of a record!'

Jo smiled, rather warily.

'Oh, cheer up!' said Elizabeth. 'It's not the end of the world . . . the First Years always get more order marks than anyone else.'

'They didn't under Gerry,' muttered Jo.

'No, well, Gerry's a bit of a tyrant, isn't she?'

'They only voted me in 'cause they wanted to get rid of her. They only did it for a joke.'

'Did they indeed? Well, I'll tell you what –' Elizabeth had looked rather more closely, now, at the order mark graph – 'why not turn the tables? Make the joke on them – show them that you can be a tyrant just as well as Gerry. That'll shake them! Certainly something's got to be done about it . . . a joke's a joke, but we're never going to win the Cup if they carry on like that.'

'I just wanted to say,' said Jo, addressing Matty and the Bookends, along with Barge, Bozzy and Fij next morning before assembly, 'that we're never going to win the Cup if we carry on like that.'

There was a silence. Barge put her head under her desk lid and gave an ostentatious hum. Bozzy dived into her school bag and pretended to be rootling for something. Matty, turning to the room at large, for all the world as if Jo had never spoken, said brightly, 'You done your letters to Prole?'

'We've done ours,' said Emma. 'Do you want to know what we've said? I've said, Dear Proline –'

'It's Pauline,' said Jo, 'actually.'

'What?' Emma stopped. 'What's Pauline?'

'Her name.'

'Her *name*?'

'Yes.'

'*Pauline*?'

'Yes.'

'So why've we been calling her Proline?'

'You idiot!' screeched Barge. She banged down her desk lid and turned on the hapless Bozzy. 'Trust you to go and get it wrong!'

'How was I to know?' said Bozzy, aggrieved. 'It *looked* like Proline.'

'How could it have been?' fumed Barge. 'What kind of a name is Proline?'

'It could have been. People *are* called peculiar names. Look at that girl in the Fifth that's called Grizzle. You can't get much more peculiar than that.'

'That's because she's foreign, you halfwit!'

'This is grotesque,' said Emma. She looked at Bozzy, sternly. 'We've all been going round addressing her as Prole!'

'Yes,' said Matty, 'and we've all written *Dear Proline*.'

'And you *know* what Miss Lloyd's like about crossings out.'

'She'll think we've all done it on purpose to be funny.'

'She'll be furious!'

'Well, don't blame *me*.' Bozzy dumped her bag self-righteously on top of her desk. 'Blame *her*.' She nodded, bug-eyed, in Jo's direction. 'If she knew, why didn't she tell us?'

'Yes! That's right!'

They rounded, accusingly, on Jo.

'If you knew, why didn't you tell us?'

'Just letting us go on making fools of ourselves –'

'I would have thought,' said Barge, bitterly, 'that people who had sworn an oath of allegiance to people might have been expected to be loyal to those people, not just stand about sneering while they made spectacles of themselves. Do pardon me,' said Barge, hugely and heavily sarcastic, 'if I have got it wrong. I rather thought that was what it was all about, an oath of allegiance. Please tell me, someone, where I have gone astray!'

'Where we have all gone astray –' Fij said it soberly –

'was in voting Jammy form captain. It's gone and divided her loyalties.'

'Oh, really!' Barge made a trumpeting sound down her nostrils. 'Is that what you call it? Personally I'd call it downright treachery.'

'Especially,' said Bozzy, viciously, 'as we're all going to have to redo our letters and it took me hours and *hours* to write it legibly.'

'Give it to me,' said Jo, eager to make a peace offering. 'I'll do it for you.'

'Give it to you?' Bozzy looked at her, haughtily (as haughtily as a small-sized person with pop eyes and a snub nose *could* look). 'I wouldn't give you the snot out of my nose!'

8

'Whose stuff is this lying around?' demanded Jo, picking a bag up off the floor. 'Is it yours?'

She glared at the Lollipop, who was busy stuffing her face as usual.

'Might be,' said the Lollipop. 'Might not be. What's it to you?' She thought she was being cheeky, in the way that Nadge could be, but in fact, thought Jo, she was merely being insolent.

'What it is to *me*,' said Jo, 'is a bit of junk left in a place where it oughtn't to be, and if you don't know whose it is I'll go and put it in Lost Property.'

Lol choked, splatting bits of crisp about her desk lid. 'Let's have a look . . . it might be mine.'

'Too late!' Jo swung the bag out of reach and marched smartly from the room with it. She would show that Lollipop! She would show all of them . . . you didn't mess with Jo Jameson.

'Jammeeeeeeee!' Lol screeched it at her, the length of the corridor. 'Bring that bag back!'

Jo continued serenely on her way. Next second and she heard the Lollipop flip-flopping flat-footedly down the corridor in pursuit of her, still screeching at the top of her voice.

'You gimme that bag! You got no right!'

'Laurel Bustamente! What do you think you're doing,

87

running in the corridor?'

Jo risked a quick glance over her shoulder and saw an outraged Wendy Armstrong, hands on hips, confronting a heaving Lollipop. Good! Now she would get her comeuppance.

The prefect in charge of Lost Property was Pauline Marsh (it was very difficult not to think of her as Proline). She looked puzzled when Jo handed in the bag.

'But this says Laurel Bustamente! I thought she was in your form?'

'Yes, she is,' said Jo.

'So why are you bringing her bag to Lost Prop?'

'To teach her a lesson,' said Jo.

There were some prefects who would have told her pretty sharply that Lost Property wasn't there to teach people lessons, it was there for lost property; Pauline only shrugged a shoulder.

'You know she'll have to pay 5p to get it out again?'

'That's all right,' said Jo. That would teach her another lesson. It would teach her that being impertinent to form captains came expensive. She was just about sick of getting a load of bad mouth from totally insignificant people such as the Lollipop and Melanie. Even Ash had tried it on the other day, and Ash was just about as insignificant as you could get.

On her way back along the lower corridor she crossed paths with Wendy Armstrong.

'I do wish,' said Wendy, in complaining tones, 'that you would keep your lot in better order.'

'I'm doing my best!' snapped Jo.

Wendy looked at her in surprise. Jo was usually one of the more respectful of the First Years.

'Sorry I spoke, I'm sure,' said Wendy.

Nag nag nag, thought Jo. She was trying; what more could she do?

As she reached the form room she saw Miss Lloyd approaching from the opposite direction. She scuttled inside, quickly, and clapped her hands.

'Miss Lloyd's coming!'

Melanie, rudely, said 'So what?' and continued to brush her hair. Nadge, standing on her desk lid, giggled and flipped a rubber at Barge, who promptly scooped it up and hurled it back.

'Stop it!' said Jo.

Bozzy said, 'She's off again!' and everybody groaned. The Lollipop said, 'I'm going to tell Miss Lloyd what you did with my bag.' Nadge threw her rubber up at the ceiling, making Naomi scream as it landed on her head. The Bookends, noisily, were doing one of their double acts. Matty was hanging out of the window yelling at someone. Jo hesitated, torn between letting them get on with it and taking a stand, showing them that she meant business. Whichever she did – or didn't do – she was going to make herself unpopular with someone, either with the rest of the form or with Miss Lloyd.

Power, reflected Jo, was really very isolating. She wondered whether the Queen felt isolated. Of course, it was different for the Queen; she was only a figurehead. She didn't actually have to go around giving the orders and telling people to stop doing things they liked and start doing things they didn't like. The Queen was popular. Mrs Thatcher hadn't been popular. No one liked Mrs Thatcher. But then Mrs Thatcher was bossy and strident. All Jo did was *ask* people, *nicely*. She was never strident. She never lost her temper, or yelled at them, or –

'STOP THAT!' bawled Jo, as Nadge's rubber went hurtling past, dangerously close to her left ear. She rubbed at her earlobe, incensed. 'Everybody just SHUT UP and sit down!'

To her amazement, everybody did. There were mutterings and mumblings, but they actually obeyed. Gerry sniffed, rather coldly – sarcasm had been Gerry's weapon: she had rarely had to raise her voice. Jo didn't care. She had exercised authority and it had worked!

As Miss Lloyd entered the classroom, there was an almost unnatural hush (unnatural for 1N, that is). Miss Lloyd looked at them sharply, as if suspecting trouble.

'Everything all right?' she said. Jo nodded happily, and skipped to her seat. 'Good! That makes a change. Yes, what is it, Laurel?'

'Please can I go and get my bag out of Lost Prop. before it closes? Otherwise –' the Lollipop shot a malicious glance in Jo's direction – 'I shan't be able to hand in my homework.'

'Rather careless of you,' commented Miss Lloyd, 'losing a bag so early in the day.'

'I didn't lose it.' The Lollipop's voice was full of venom and self-righteousness. Now Jo would be for it! '*She* took it.'

'Who is She? I don't know anyone by the name of She.'

'Jam,' said the Lollipop.

'Me,' said Jo. She sprang up, defiantly, from her desk. 'I took it 'cause it had been left lying around where someone could have tripped over it and broken their neck.'

'Yes, and you knew perfectly well whose it was 'cause it's got my name on it!'

'I asked you,' said Jo. 'You said you didn't know.'

'I said –' The Lollipop stopped. 'I said it *might* be. If you'd let me look, I could've told you.'

'I should have thought,' said Miss Lloyd, crisply, 'that you would have been able to recognize your own bag at a glance – unless there are a dozen others like it?'

There wasn't even one other like it. Lol's bag was highly distinctive: her Italian aunt had brought it over for her on her last visit. It was red canvas, with embroidered flowers and the word *Firenze*, which was Italian for Florence. Everyone knew Lol's bag.

'I suggest,' said Miss Lloyd, 'that you go and redeem it and that in future you don't leave it lying around.'

The Lollipop flolloped out, her face crimson with fury and indignation.

'Honestly,' whispered Fij reproachfully to Jo, 'that is the most terrible favouritism.'

Jo refuted the suggestion indignantly. It wasn't anything to do with favouritism! Miss Lloyd knew that Jo had only been doing her duty, as she had promised to do, and that Lol had cheeked her. Lol had got no more than she deserved. All the same, at breaktime Lol made the most of it and 1N were inclined to agree with Fij.

'Now she's teacher's pet!' said the Mouse. 'That's *all* we need.'

When Jo had started at Peter High she had been nothing and no one: a nonentity. By the end of her first term, what with being in the Under-13s netball and taking part in the House play, she had been *al*most somebody; and then in her second term she had become part of the Laing Gang (Bozzy, Jammy, Fij and Barge) and thus a Person to Be Reckoned with. She had been popular. People liked her. They had clamoured to sit next to her, to partner her, to seek her opinion. Now they seemed almost to hate her. Well, perhaps hate was too strong, but they were definitely resentful.

'It is a bit much,' said Barge, 'making Lol fork out 5p when you must have *known* it was her bag.'

'Well, if I knew it,' retorted Jo, 'so did she!'

'Of course she did. That's not the point.'

'So what is the point?'

'The point is,' said Bozzy, 'that you've been mean and unfair to the poor Lollipop.'

Poor Lollipop? Last term, Barge and Bozzy hadn't been able to *stand* the Lollipop. They had even thrown her out of the Gang, just so they could bring Jo in in her place. (A horrible thought occurred to Jo: suppose they now threw her out and reinstated the Lollipop?)

'You really are chucking your weight around,' said Barge, 'rather too much.'

It sounded, to Jo's ears, like a threat. It seemed to be saying, just watch it . . .

'We shall have to start up a fund,' said Barge. 'Like people do when people are fined and they don't think it's right . . . they start up funds and collect the money for them.'

'That's a good idea,' said Bozzy. She tucked her arm through Barge's. 'Demonstrate solidity.'

'You mean solidarity,' said Jo.

'I mean what I mean!' screeched Bozzy.

'Yes, just stop trying to be so *clever* all the time. It's bad enough bossing people without squashing them as well.'

'Exactly. If we'd wanted someone clever we'd have voted for Gerry.'

'Who is *really* clever.'

'Let's go and start the fund,' said Bozzy. She turned to Fij. 'Coming?'

Fij hesitated. She was Jo's friend, but she had been a member of the Laing Gang ever since the Homestead. Jo could see that it was difficult for her.

'I'd better just go along and supervise.' She looked at Jo apologetically. 'Just to make sure they spell things right.'

Jo watched the three of them, arms linked, go walking off across the playground. She could hardly go with them, to demonstrate solidarity with someone whose bag she had purposely put into Lost Property to teach them a lesson; and in any case she hadn't been invited.

Jo sighed. She would have given anything to be back in the carefree days of last term, unburdened by responsibility. The trouble with responsibility was that once you'd got it there didn't seem to be any honourable way that you could get rid of it again, even though you didn't want it and had never asked for it.

The days jogged on towards half term. Good things happened, and bad things happened. Amongst the bad things were:

1) Barge, Bozzy and the Bookends standing in the playground for the whole of one lunch break shaking an empty jam jar and holding aloft a piece of card which said HELP BEAT INJUSTICE! *Contribute to the Bag Fund* in large red letters, so that naturally

everyone kept coming up and wanting to know what it was about, which Barge etc. took great delight in telling them, with the result that by the end of the lunch break they had collected almost 20p (they ostentatiously announced that they would keep the extra 15p to fight future injustice) and everyone seemed to think that Jo was the most frightful tyrant. Lol, needless to say, was cock-a-hoop.

2) Jo overhearing Melanie talking to Ash about the Laing Gang and speculating who would be in it next term instead of Jo.

3) Jo telling Claire *yet again* to stop practising her ballet in the cloakroom and Claire refusing, which meant Jo having no option but to report her, because if she didn't then it would be her who got the blame when Claire was discovered (which sooner or later she was bound to be), and so Jo had chosed Kay Wyman, who after all was Head of the House, and all Kay had done was laugh and say, 'Oh, Claire! We tend to turn a blind eye to her. There's not much you can do with someone who's so determinedly single-minded.' Jo had felt humiliated. They might at least have *told* her.

Amongst the good things were:

1) Katy Wells of the Second Year spraining her ankle and Jo taking her place in the Under-14s cricket against York and actually *scoring* (she only got fifteen runs, but then loads of people got even less, the whole side being out for fifty-two, so that all in all she felt she hadn't done too badly, especially as York were out for a mere forty-five).

2) 1N playing 1S at rounders and Jo getting three rounders (Nadge got five, but then Nadge was Nadge).

3) The school mag. coming out and Jo being the only person from 1N other than Gerry, who had written a long boring piece about ancient burial mounds, to have had anything printed (Barge and Bozzy, who sometimes, these days, weren't on speaking terms with her, now hummed and hahed and wondered if it was quite as good as they had originally thought, but Fij stoutly maintained that it was 'absolutely brilliant' and by far the best thing in there).

4) Attending a House meeting with Nadge and being publicly congratulated by Kay Wyman, in front of *all* the rest of the House reps, *including* the two snotty noses from the Second Year, because for the first time in living memory the First Years had managed to exist for an entire week without incurring one single order mark.

'Well done!' Elizabeth came up at the end of the meeting and cordially biffed Jo on the shoulder. 'You've obviously shaken them!'

Jo was pleased that Elizabeth was pleased, but she could have wished she hadn't come and biffed her and said what she did in front of Nadge; she noticed that Nadge was giving her some really funny looks. The Second Years, needless to say, were consumed with jealousy. Whereas before they had denounced the First Years as too young to be treated as responsible human beings, and the sort of people who would vote for a pop star as Prime Minister, they now started jeering (just because Kay had suggested they might try taking a leaf out of the First Years' book) and calling them Holy Hildas and mealy-mouthed little pompous goody-goody prigs.

Wendy Armstrong caught up with Nadge and Jo as they were leaving the meeting.

'I'm glad you took my advice to heart,' she said, nodding approvingly at Jo. 'Keep it up and we might really be in with a chance.'

'What's she on about?' said Nadge, when Wendy was safely out of earshot.

'Oh!' Jo hunched a shoulder, trying to make light of it. 'She had a go at me the other day when Lol was running in the corridor.'

'Had a go at *you*?'

'Well, because of me being form captain . . . and then Elizabeth saw the order marks list and said we'd have to do something about it if we wanted to stand any chance of winning the Cup.' It hadn't happened quite that way round, but she wanted Nadge to know that she'd been got at: that it hadn't been *her* idea to start bossing people.

Nadge was silent awhile, frowning and running a finger along the wood panelling of the corridor.

'Of course,' she said, 'it's going to be games that *really* counts.'

'Oh, well, of *course*,' said Jo. She didn't want to upset Nadge; Nadge was almost the only person who hadn't shown any resentment towards her.

'We always come top of the cricket, and if we can manage to win the junior rounders –'

'Which I'm sure we *shall*,' gushed Jo.

96

The interhouse rounders tournament, senior and junior sections, was held on the last Saturday of term. Jo was looking forward to it. The tournament went on for the whole morning. All the Houses played one another in their own year groups, then the winners from the individual years went on to the finals. Jo was so certain of her place on the team that she had already arranged with Robbie that he would come along and watch.

She became aware that Nadge was studying her.

'I didn't just mean winning *our section*,' said Nadge. 'I meant actually winning the *Junior Shield*.'

Jo said, 'Gosh!' which was a silly sort of thing to say, but she wasn't used to the easygoing Nadge being that ambitious. 'The Junior *Shield*?'

That would mean beating both Second Years and Third. It had on very rare occasions happened that all three finalists in each section had come from the same House, but what had never happened was a First Year team ending up overall winner of the junior section.

'We can but try,' said Nadge, 'and we have got a jolly strong team.' She began ticking them off on her fingers. 'You, me, Fij – Barge, Bozzy, the Bookends –'

'Matty,' said Jo. She still remained loyal to Matty from their days at Juniors together; and they were still friends at weekends and during holidays.

'Matty,' agreed Nadge. 'Gerry. Claire if she would *play* –'

'I don't think she will,' said Jo. 'She has her ballet exams.'

'Well, we don't really need her; only as reserve. And there's always Melanie and Ash if *all* else fails.'

'Melanie wouldn't be too bad,' said Jo, 'if only she'd put some effort into it.'

'Neither would Lol if she could only move a bit faster.'

It was quite like old times to be ambling down the corridor discussing team places with Nadge; Jo almost managed to forget that she was form captain and had responsibilities. It wasn't until they reached the playground and she was treated to the unedifying spectacle of the Bookends hanging upside down, side by side, like a pair of bats, showing all their knickers, from one of the branches of the big chestnut tree which overhung the wire netting, that it was forcibly brought back to her. People weren't *supposed* to hang upside down from the chestnut tree. If they went and fell off and broke their stupid necks, it would be all Jo's fault. Everyone would say, 'You're form captain; why didn't you stop them?'

Jo was about to go across and ask them – very patiently and gently, so they couldn't take offence – if they would kindly mind unhooking themselves and coming back down into the playground, when Nadge gave a great gleeful whoop and went capering over to join them. Before Jo knew it, Nadge, too, was hanging upside down like a bat . . .

I give up, thought Jo. I just give *up*. If anyone caught them, it was just too bad.

On Friday, at the Youth Club, Mrs Barlow (the lady who ran it) wanted them to play a game called goosey, which she said she had played when she was their age.

'*Goosey*?' bellowed Tom, and one or two of the bigger boys sniggered.

Jo gave Tom a shove. Matty, politely, said, 'How d'you play it, miss?'

How you played it was, you all sat round in a circle

except for one person who was goosey. This person that was goosey then prowled round the outside until they suddenly touched someone on the shoulder (shouting 'Goosey!' as they did so) and ran like the wind in an attempt to get round the circle and back to the beginning before the person that had been touched managed to catch up with them. If they succeeded, then they took the person's place and the other person became goosey instead of them.

There was a silence as Mrs Barlow finished explaining; then Tom said, 'That's the game?'

'Yes,' said Mrs Barlow. 'I know it doesn't sound much but it's great fun and gives you lots of exercise.'

'It's for *babies*,' said Tom. 'Why can't we watch a video?'

'Because I'm afraid I haven't brought one,' said Mrs Barlow.

'You promised!' roared Tom.

'No, she didn't.' There were times when Jo really despaired of Tom's manners. 'She said she would if she could, and I think goosey sounds a really nice game and *I* want to play it even if you don't.'

'No, I don't!' said Tom.

'Well, you're jolly well going to,' said Jo, ''cause everyone else is!'

'Who says?'

'Mrs Barlow says – and so do I.'

'And what have you got to do with it?'

'Nothing,' said Matty. 'She hasn't got nothing to do with it, she's just being bossy again. She's really getting like Margaret Thatcher.'

'Tom! Matty! Please,' said Mrs Barlow. 'Don't let's

have a slanging match. Those who want to play can play, the rest can go off and do their own thing. I'm not here to force people. Hands up the ones who want to play?'

Jo put her hand up; so, she was relieved to see, did Robbie. So, after a second, did Jool and Matty. Then Nadge put hers up (Nadge couldn't resist anything which meant running and chasing) and as soon as she did that everyone else put their hands up, too – everyone except Tom. Tom couldn't very well, after all the rude fuss that he'd made. Mrs Barlow said, 'Sure you don't want to change your mind, Tom?' but he only scowled and shook his head and said 'I'd sooner go home,' and so he did and was in the most terrifically evil temper when Jo got back.

He greeted her at the door with 'Stupid Thatcher bitch!'

'Don't you call me that!' shrieked Jo.

'Thatcher Thatcher Thatcher!' shouted Tom.

Jo hurled herself at him. Tom, trying to defend himself, caught Jo in the eye with his elbow. Jo screamed and kicked, Tom bellowed, the telephone was knocked off its perch and went crashing to the floor.

'What the hell is going on?' roared Andy, appearing at the door of the sitting room. (It was a night, fortunately, when their parents were out and Andy was being bribed with vast sums of money to stay indoors and keep an eye on them.)

'He called me Thatcher,' sobbed Jo, holding a hand-kerchief to her eye.

'Thatcher! Hitler! Mussolini! Attila the Hun! Gengiz K –'

'Stop that!' yelled Andy, taking a swipe.

Tom, ducking adroitly under his brother's flailing

arm, fled to the top of the stairs, from the comparative safety of which he turned and bawled, '*Bossy*boots! *Bossy*boots!' before charging along the passage to his bedroom and loudly slamming the door.

'What on earth have you been up to?' said Andy, removing the handkerchief from Jo's eye. 'That's going to be black in the morning. He didn't hit you, did he?'

'N-not on p-purpose, but he c-called me n-names!'

'So I heard,' said Andy. 'Why?'

"Cause of me being f-form captain and everyone s-saying that I b-boss them.'

'And do you?'

'Not more'n I have to.'

'So how much do you have to?'

'Well –' Jo screwed her handkerchief into a ball. 'Quite a lot, I s'ppose, but they don't take any notice if I ask them nicely, and I'm the one that gets the blame when we get nine million order marks. And it's all right everyone going on about the blasted Cup all the time, but they never stop and think how we're s'pposed to stand a chance of winning if they're just going to keep doing things they shouldn't, so in the end I just have to yell at them.'

'And what happens when you yell at them? Apart from them saying you're bossy . . . does it have any effect?'

'Yes, it does,' said Jo, "cause this week they didn't get any order marks at *all* and that is a *record*.'

'So have you congratulated them?'

'Well – n-no. I s'ppose I haven't, actually.'

'Don't you think you ought?'

'Mm.' Jo scrubbed at her nose. 'I s'ppose so.'

'I think you ought,' said Andy. 'I think it's something they'd be pretty pleased about.'

'All right,' said Jo. She cheered up. 'I'll do it on Monday.'

9

'What's this?' said Barge, coming into the classroom on Monday morning. She stopped in front of the board. *'Congratulations 1N, no order marks last week, very well done?'*

'Patronizing *cow*,' said Melanie.

'Cheek!'

'Nerve!'

'Who *does* she think she is?'

Jo, sitting in her desk at the back, opened up her desk lid and tried to pretend she wasn't there. She could feel her cheeks pulsating. How unfair they were! She wasn't being patronizing, she had just wanted them to know that she was pleased with them. You'd have thought they'd be happy about it, not all grudging and resentful.

'No order marks last week –' Melanie did a silly little prance about the room. 'So what do we get? A gold star?'

'We might get the Cup,' said Jo, 'if we carry on.'

That shut them up, at any rate momentarily: they obviously hadn't noticed that she was there.

'Well, yes, we *might*,' said Barge. 'But there again –' she brought it out with an air of triumph– 'there again, it has to be said, we might *not*.'

'Precisely,' said Bozzy.

'And in the meantime,' said Melanie, flouncing

rather, 'we can do without being patronized, thank you very much.'

'Even the prefects don't *patronize*.'

'And they,' said Bozzy, who had a talent for stating the obvious, 'are prefects.'

'Precisely,' said Barge. 'They are in a *position* to patronize. Jammy is only one of us and no better than anyone else.'

'If as good,' urged the Lollipop. (She was still feeling vindictive after the affair of the bag, even though the Bag Fund had paid her fine.)

'*If* as good,' agreed Bozzy.

'What, after all, is her contribution?' wondered Barge. 'Is *she* going to win the First Year prize for Overall Performance?'

Bozzy sniggered. 'Shouldn't think so!'

'Is *she* going to come top of First Year exams?'

'Not unless my name is Princess Diana.'

'Which it isn't,' said Barge.

'Precisely,' said Bozzy. She nodded, with the air of one who had scored a point.

'So what is she throwing her weight about for?'

'Just because she was voted form captain –'

'As a *joke* –'

'– she needn't think she can start treating us as if we are children.'

'It's almost enough,' said Melanie, 'to make you want to get order marks on purpose.'

'It is certainly very vexatious,' said Barge – she looked at Jo, sternly – 'when a person who is *no* better than anyone else chooses to set herself up as being in some way *above* them.'

'Jammy didn't set herself up,' objected Fij. 'We did.'

'Yes: as a *joke*.'

'As she very well knows.'

'I suppose –' Fij glanced worriedly at Jo as she said it – 'I suppose perhaps it may have seemed like a joke to *us*, but not to Jam.'

'Oh, well! If you're going to take *that* line. . . . I put it to you,' said Barge, grandly, 'is it our fault she has no sense of humour?'

'It's not that I haven't got a sense of humour,' said Jo, earnestly, as she and Fij walked round the playground together at break. 'I *have* got a sense of humour. It's just that you can't be form captain as a joke, it doesn't work that way.'

'No-o-o. . . .' Fij said it thoughtfully. 'It would have been better, really, if Miss Lloyd had taken the badge off you right at the beginning.'

Would it? There were moments (such as this morning) when Jo almost felt that Fij was right; but then there were other moments (such as when Elizabeth had said well done and Kay had publicly congratulated her) when she wasn't so sure.

'I suppose you could always resign,' said Fij.

That was what Tom had suggested. Couldn't they see that resigning meant admitting defeat? Robbie could see it; why couldn't Fij and Tom?

'If I resigned,' said Jo, 'we'd have Gerry back again.'

'Yes, but at least we're used to Gerry. I mean, people *expect* her to boss them around; they don't expect you to.'

'I don't mean to boss,' said Jo, miserably.

'Well, this is it,' said Fij. 'This is what I keep trying to tell them . . . she doesn't *mean* to. I expect it's because you're new to it,' said Fij, kindly. 'That's what it is.'

Jo rubbed a finger along her forehead. There was something wrong with Fij's argument. She suddenly realized what it was: 'Gerry's not new to it,' she said, 'and *she* bosses. You just said so!'

'Yes, but Gerry –' Fij explained it patiently, as if to someone not very bright – 'Gerry is Gerry: you are you. You used to be such *fun*!' said Fij. 'It gets awfully boring when you keep going on at people all the time.'

'It's quite boring for me, too,' said Jo.

'Then why do it? Why not just . . . hang loose!' said Fij.

Jo thought about it. 'I'm not sure Miss Lloyd would be very pleased if I just hung loose.' Nor would Elizabeth. Nor would Wendy. Nor would Kay. 'We'd get simply mounds of order marks and I'd be the one they put the blame on.'

'Yes,' Fij frowned. 'I can see that is a problem. Really and truly there is only one solution, and that is for you to go to Miss Lloyd and hand in your badge.'

'I can't,' said Jo. 'She won't let me.'

'Won't *let* you? She can't not let you! That'd be like – like the Queen saying she wanted to stop being Queen and the Prime Minister telling her she couldn't.'

There was a pause while Jo considered the picture that Fij's words conjured up.

'That doesn't seem a very likely sort of thing,' said Jo.

'Well, exactly,' said Fij.

'No, but I mean . . . she's the *Queen*.'

'I know she's the Queen! That's what I said.'

'*I*'m not,' said Jo.

'That's right,' said Fij, soothingly. 'You're not.'

'Well, then –'

'Well, then!'

Jo rubbed a finger up her nose. She seemed to be missing something.

'I've got lost,' she said. 'What are we talking about?'

'About you being the Queen.'

'No! Before that.'

'You said you wanted to resign –'

'I said I *couldn't* resign.'

'Yes, and then I said –'

The argument continued, amiably, and on the whole somewhat mindlessly, all the way round the playground. By the time the bell rang for the end of break they had almost forgotten the original subject of their discussion. Jo only remembered it as they went up the steps into school and heard Michelle Wandres snap, 'Margery Laing and Chloë Boswood! If you don't stop heaving and pushing you can both take an order mark.' Fij looked at Jo and pulled a face. Jo, rather urgently, whispered, 'Nobody ever asked *me* if I wanted to be form captain!'

'That is true,' said Fij.

They walked, ostentatiously quiet and in single file, past Michelle, who glared at them as if she would have liked to find fault and was peeved that she couldn't (seconds later they heard her yelling at Katy Wells to 'stop filling your fat face in the corridor!') and continued in the wake of Barge and Bozzy towards their form room. Bozzy turned at the last minute and saw them. She gave Barge a hefty shove.

107

'Quick!' shrieked Bozzy. 'Here comes Bossy Boots!'

Barge and Bozzy hurled themselves, panting and snorting, through the door.

'It's a pity,' said Fij, 'that we didn't pick someone *really* useless, like the Lollipop. But then,' she added, 'if we'd picked the Lollipop no one would ever have voted for her. Not even as a joke.'

Jo supposed that in her own muddled way Fij was trying to make things better.

As they opened the door of the form room everyone stopped what they were doing and scuttled for their desks. A curious buzzing noise filled the air. It sounded like, 'Bozbuz, Bozbuz.' It took Jo a second or so to realize that what it was was 1N hissing, 'Bossyboots, Bossyboots.' It was Fij who blushed, not Jo. Jo marched determinedly, looking neither to right nor to left, up the gangway to her own desk at the back.

After a moment, when the hissing had died away, the Lollipop put up her hand and in a silly little-girly-type voice lisped, 'Please, miss, is it all right if I ask someone a question? I don't want to get an order mark, miss.'

Several people tittered. Jo said, 'Are you talking to me?'

'Yes, miss. 'Cause you're in charge, aren't you, miss?'

'So what do you want?' said Jo.

'I want to ask the stationery monitor a question, miss.' Jo shrugged.

'Can I, miss? Oh, *thank* you, miss!' The Lollipop turned, effusively, to Emma. 'I wonder if I might trouble you for a new writing block?'

'But of *course*,' gushed Emma. 'I shall be only too delighted.'

Emma sprang out of her desk with the alacrity of one who has only been awaiting the word and went bouncing over to the stationery cupboard. She turned the handle of the door: nothing happened. She wrenched at it: still nothing happened. She banged it, rattled it, pounded on it. Then she turned, distraught, to Jo.

'Jam*meeeee*! Help! The door is stuck!'

'Oh, *quick*! Hurry!' gasped the Mouse. 'Miss Briarley will be here any second and if we're not ready for her –'

'ORDER MARKS!' The class chanted it in unison (all except for Fij and Jo).

Jo wasn't daft: she knew they were having a laugh at her expense, but what could she do? It was quite true that Miss Briarley would be here at any second, and they *were* supposed to be ready and waiting.

Impatiently, Jo walked up to the stationery cupboard and gave the door a tug. It came open quite easily – so easily, in fact, that Jo went staggering backwards, into Claire's desk. As she did so, out of the stationery cupboard poured forth stationery: books, pads, pens, in vast profusion: boxes of chalks, spare registers, flower pots, vases, all the bits and pieces which tend to accumulate in stationery cupboards, tumbled across the floor.

'*Oh*!' squeaked the Mouse, highly excited.

'Now see what you've gone and done,' said the Lollipop.

'So careless,' twittered Ash.

'Just *look* at it –'

'All *over* the place –'

'All I wanted was a writing block,' said Lol. She snickered. 'I didn't ask for all that lot!'

'Doesn't know her own strength,' gloated Melanie.

'The door *felt* stuck,' said Emma.

'Oh, now, look!' Fij started up out of her desk. 'Everybody help put it back – and whoever did it, own up!'

'Did what?' said Emma, wide-eyed.

'Piled all the stationery up. You're not being fair! Jammy didn't ask to be form captain – we're the ones that made her. You don't think *she* likes it, do you?'

There was a bit of muttering – some of it abashed, some rebellious – then Nadge came bounding out of her seat, quickly followed by Claire, and started gathering up the scattered stationery. Soon all the class were scrabbling on the floor. The last stick of chalk had just been returned to its box as Miss Briarley appeared.

Later that day, Barge, Bozzy and the Bookends came up to Jo as she was collecting her blazer from the cloakroom.

'Look here, we're a deputation,' said Barge.

'We have come to deputate,' said Bozzy.

'You keep out of it!' Barge turned on her. 'I'll do the talking. There's no such word as deputate.'

'Bet there is!'

'Bet there isn't!'

'You ask Jammy! She'll tell you.'

'Is there?' said Barge.

'Um – I don't think so,' said Jo.

'See?'

'She only said she didn't think so. She d –'

'Oh, shut up!' said Barge. 'Now, what we have decided,' she announced, in magisterial fashion, to Jo, 'is that if you will stop bossing us we will do our best to stop getting quite so many order marks – not, of course, that we got any at *all* last week, as you so generously reminded us.'

'But that,' said the Mouse, hurriedly, 'was probably a sort of fluke.'

'Yes; we can't guarantee to be on our best behaviour *all* of the time. But if you will stop bossing, we will at least try. I don't think we can say fairer than that.'

'*Definitely* not,' said Bozzy. 'Indubitably not. Und –'

Barge looked at her. 'Do you mind? I am the one who is conducting these negotiations.' She turned back to Jo. 'Those are our terms. Do you accept them or not? Nod once if you do and twice if you don't.'

'Or just say yes or no,' said Bozzy.

'*Will* you shut up?' said Barge, testily. 'We can do without your tinny little voice constantly yammering away. This is a Historic Moment.'

It certainly wasn't the moment for pointing out that if 1N hadn't amassed order marks by the ton in the first place, there would never have been any need for Jo to boss (not that she *had* bossed).

Slowly, she nodded her head.

'Well, *that*'s a relief,' said Emma. Confidentially, to Jo, she said, 'You were becoming frightfully tiresome.'

'I'm sorry,' said Jo, humbly.

'That's all right; we could see you couldn't help it. It was our fault,' said Emma, magnanimously, 'for electing someone without any sense of humour.'

'Next time, perhaps –' Jo couldn't resist the temptation – 'we should vote for Barge.'

'Ye-e-e-e-s . . .'

She could see that Emma wasn't sure how to take the

111

suggestion. Was Jo serious? Or had she perhaps got a sense of humour after all?

Joyfully, Jo snatched her blazer off the peg. With any luck the second half of term might just about be bearable.

10

Over half term Jo: went to a cricket match with Andy and her dad; went shopping with her mum; attended special acrobatic dancing classes in the church hall (every afternoon for four days); went to the Water Palace with Matty (twice); went out with Robbie (once for a walk, once to the cinema, once up to town to visit a museum). She also: read six books, bought the latest single by Bo Peep and the Bad Boys (currently her favourite group: Tom said they were *yuck*) and wrote a poem about an ant that was voted Top Ant of the Ant Heap but really just wanted to be an ordinary ant the same as everyone else.

She thought of the ant poem when she was sitting in the garden the day before going back to school. She wasn't exactly *worried* about going back to school, but she couldn't help a few twinges of apprehension. Suppose Barge and the Bookends forgot the pact that they had made? Suppose the rest of the form didn't go along with it? Suppose they all started misbehaving and getting order marks again? She most desperately didn't want to be unpopular, but neither did she want to disappoint Miss Lloyd or let down Elizabeth.

Robbie, when told of her dilemma, said, 'It sounds to me as if they're taking advantage.'

They were, of course – taking advantage had been the

113

whole point of voting for her in the first place – but that didn't really help in knowing how to deal with the situation.

'Maybe,' said Robbie, 'things'll be all right now you've had it out with them.'

Jo could only hope so, because otherwise she couldn't think what she was going to do.

First thing Monday morning, as she walked into the classroom, Melanie sang, 'Watch out! There's a Bossyboots about!' Jo's heart sank: it was starting all over again.

'I saw Bossy walking in the park . . . she was with her *boyfriend*: they were holding *hands*.'

'Oooooh! Bossyboots!'

'Now, look here!' Barge came bustling self-importantly down the gangway. 'We're not calling her that anymore! She's Jammy again.'

Jo looked at her, gratefully; Barge really wasn't so bad, under all the bluster. Melanie flounced a bit. The Lollipop, resentful, said, 'Who says so?'

'*I* say so,' said Barge. 'We *all* say so.' She flung out a hand, embracing Fij, Bozzy and the Bookends. 'We've come to an agreement: Jam's going to stop bossing and we're going to stop getting quite so many order marks.'

'Ho! *Are* we?' Melanie pulled some books out of her bag and slapped them down on to her desk lid. 'Well, it's news to me, that's all I can say.'

'And I really don't see,' muttered Lol, under her breath, 'what right they've got to go deciding things for the rest of us.'

They hadn't any right, other than lack of natural predators: few people dared oppose the Laing Gang,

114

especially when teamed up with Emma and the Mouse. Gerry & Co. were the only force strong enough to withstand them, but for once Gerry and the Laing Gang were likely to be in agreement. Jo couldn't see Gerry siding with the lawbreakers. As for the rest, Jool and Matty tended to follow (and besides, Matty was Jo's friend), Claire was too wrapped up in her ballet to care one way or the other, Nadge was a law unto herself whoever was in authority. That only left Melanie and Ash, and the Lollipop, and nobody ever took any notice of them. Things were definitely looking up.

'But you've got to keep to your side of the bargain,' warned Barge. 'We don't want any more of that Mrs Thatcher stuff.'

Jo promised, humbly, that there wouldn't be.

'In that case,' said Barge, magnanimous in her hour of victory, 'we shall do our best to at least keep the order marks down below the level of that hideous loathsome scum in the Second Year. More than that I cannot guarantee. But one in the eye for *them* is not something to be sneezed at, I think you will agree.'

'Oh yes, I *do*,' said Jo. 'Absolutely!'

'That is all right, then,' said Barge. 'Just so long as we know where we stand.'

For the next two weeks, peace reigned in 1N. Jo was Jammy: she was back in favour. She hit the winning rounder in a match against Sutton's and everyone applauded; her poem, in the school mag., was one of the ones chosen for a lunch-time poetry recital given by the Poetry Society; she and Nadge were included in the Under-14 cricket team for an outside game, with Fij going along as 12th man, and the whole form became very cock-a-hoop and exultant when Jo scored twenty not out and Nadge, rather than Katy Wells, was made wicket keeper in place of Laura Harris of the Third Year, who had been suddenly promoted to the Second XI.

'We really are doing awfully well,' said Barge, in tones of cosy self-congratulation.

'Running *rings* round them,' gloated Bozzy. 'They've only won two of their matches this term: we've won all of ours.'

'And not so much as a single rhyming couplet chosen for the poetry recital!'

'Rhyming what?' said Bozzy.

'Couplet,' said Barge.

'Rhyming *cutlet*?'

'That's right, dear,' Barge patted her head, in high good humour. 'Rhyming fishcakes, rhyming fillets, just brush it with oil and put it under the grill.'

'What *is* she on about?' said Bozzy.

'Poetry, dear. Don't worry your little head about it.' Barge tapped her own head with a finger. 'Not much brain,' she mouthed. 'She doesn't understand.' Aloud, in a voice like a trumpet, she proclaimed, 'We are winning *all* the honours and our behaviour is ex-*amp*lery.'

She meant exemplary, but it would have seemed churlish to correct her when 1N's behaviour had so definitely taken a turn for the better. Of course it wasn't perfect, accidents were only to be expected – but at least they *were* accidents.

Fij, for instance, couldn't *help* carving the initials *BJB* on her desk lid with the point of her compasses. Bobby-

Jo Baird was an American soap star she was in love with; and love, as she earnestly explained to Jo after Miss Lloyd had angrily denounced her as a mindless vandal and given her two order marks, had a habit of running away with you.

'There's nothing you can do about it. It sort of takes over, if you know what I mean.'

Jo did (she sometimes felt the same way about Robbie). Fij couldn't help love taking over, any more than the Mouse could help her new puppy chewing up her homework (even if it did only seem to chew Maths, which as Mrs Stanley said, as she dished out the order marks, was a pretty strange coincidence). Any more than Bozzy could help being late three mornings running because of having to go back for things she'd forgotten, or Lol being caught with a mouthful of bun when Miss Briarley asked her a question, or Claire quite blatantly not doing her set task for Home Ec. because of having extra ballet practice. Everyone knew that Bozzy was scatterbrained, and that the Lollipop couldn't stop eating, and that Claire was single-minded. It wasn't as if they were going out of their way to get order marks; it was just the normal wear and tear of school life. Also, they had exams looming on the horizon. First Year exams weren't all *that* important – as Barge, rather too heartily, kept assuring everyone – but still there was the prospect of Miss Lloyd turning nasty if one came bottom of absolutely everything, 'which I am almost bound to do!' wailed Bozzy. 'It's all right for you,' she said to Jo, 'you're one of the clever ones.'

'Me?' said Jo (secretly rather pleased but by no means convinced that Bozzy was right). 'I can't do Maths for toffee.'

117

'I can't do anything for toffee!'

Jo tried hard to think of something that Bozzy was good at. Not being able to, she said comfortingly, 'I bet I come bottom at Maths.'

'Well, you won't,' said Bozzy, ''cause I will.'

'She always does,' said Barge.

'I always do,' said Bozzy.

Jo racked her brains. 'Home Ec!' she said. 'I bet you anything you like I come bottom at Home Ec. Mrs Dyer asked me the other day if I had two left hands.'

'She asked *me* if I was training to be a heavyweight boxer,' said Barge.

'That was only because you were pummelling your pastry. You were sort of . . . *wringing it out*. I just kept dropping mine on the floor,' said Jo. 'And then I went and trod on it so she wouldn't even let me put it in the oven . . . she said it was a health hazard.'

'Mine was a health hazard,' said Bozzy. 'My dad broke a tooth on it.'

Barge cackled. Jo said, 'Yes, but Mrs Dyer wasn't to know. She'd probably have given you full marks if that had been an exam.'

'No, she wouldn't,' said Bozzy. 'She took one look at it and said, "That would make a splendid doorstop, Chloë."'

'And then you gave it to your dad?' said Fij. 'That wasn't very nice.'

'I didn't know he'd got rotten teeth, did I?'

'Well, there you are,' said Jo. 'I don't expect Mrs Dyer has rotten teeth 'cause she's younger than your dad. So if she'd actually tasted it she might quite have liked it. She couldn't even *taste* mine.'

Bozzy refused to be solaced. 'When she tasted my apple crumble she made a nose like *eeeeeurghghgh* and spat it in the sink.'

'How rude!'

'People are rude,' said Bozzy. 'Actually it was 'cause I'd put salt in instead of sugar. She said it was the most horrible thing she'd ever tasted – and you *know* how people bear grudges. She's bound to fail me just 'cause of that.'

'Well, if that's what you want,' said Barge. She shook her head at Jo. 'You must understand,' she said, 'that Bozzy has a reputation to keep up. She'd probably freak if she didn't come bottom of everything. She's one of those people who just can't handle success.'

'I see,' said Jo.

Being, herself, a person who wasn't sure that she could handle failure, she spent the week before the exams working hard at revision. Her best subject was English, but there wasn't much you could do by way of revision for English. Her next best were French and Latin; then History and Biology; then horrible Geography; and then things like Art, and Home Ec., and CDT, but they didn't really count quite so much, because you could either do them or you couldn't, and nobody could really blame you if you weren't naturally gifted. Finally, there was the dreaded Maths.

Both her mum and her dad, and even Andy, tried to help Jo with her Maths, but her dad was too impatient, her mum said that 'things had changed' since she was at school, and Andy just shook his head in bewilderment. How *could* Jo not understand when he had carefully gone over and over the same point with her? Well, she couldn't, and that was that. Her mum, in the end, told her not to worry – 'You can't be good at everything.'

Tom jeered and said, 'Girls aren't ever any good at Maths!'

'Mum was,' said Jo. Mrs Jameson was a qualified accountant.

'*Ordinary* girls,' said Tom. '*Most* girls. *You.*'

'She takes after her dad,' said Mrs Jameson. 'They're more on the arts side.'

'Yes, and dad's hardly a girl,' said Andy. 'Or is he? Are you secretly a girl, dad?'

Jo giggled. 'P'raps dad's secretly a girl and mum's secretly a man!'

'Curses!' cried Mr Jameson. 'They've rumbled us!'

Tom, suspecting he was being laughed at, shouted, 'You need Maths if you're going to get anywhere in today's society!' and slammed out of the room.

If what Tom said was true, then Jo obviously wasn't going to get anywhere at all. Comparing notes afterwards with Barge, who was reasonably numerate, she was forced to the conclusion that she had managed to beat Bozzy at her own game; she was certain to come bottom. But in English she wrote a good long essay on 'Brothers and Sisters' (Tom would have gone mad if he had seen it – 'Brothers,' wrote Jo, 'when they are young, can be tiresome and boring and stupid. It is only when they grow older that they become decent civilized human beings') and in all of the French paper there was only one bit which she couldn't translate.

'You know where it said *Quelle couleur est* and then it had a long list of things and you had to put what colour they were? I couldn't remember what *le ciel* was so I said it was *bleu. . . .* What *is ciel*?'

'Floor?' said Fij.

'Floor!' The Lollipop gave a piglike snort of derision. 'It's the same as *cielo* in Italian.'

'So what's *chaylo*?' said Jo.

'*Sky*.'

'Oh, bliss! The *chaylo* is *bleu!*'

'My *chaylo* wasn't,' said Bozzy. 'Mine was black.'

'*Black*?'

'What on earth did you think it was?'

'Didn't think it was anything,' said Bozzy. 'Never even heard of it.'

It seemed that the very minute the exams were over, 1N had a rush of blood to the head. Nadge was caught climbing up a drainpipe outside the gym – 'Just to see if I could'; the Bookends crept out of school one lunch break and were spotted in the High Street, playing Space Invaders in a Chinese takeaway; Barge was reported for 'unseemly behaviour in a public place' (i.e., pushing and jostling on a no. 514 bus); the Lollipop brought one of her dad's pizzas into school and brazenly shared it out in the middle of a Biology lesson, her, Melanie and Ash, all crouched down beneath the back bench in the lab, making disgusting eating noises; even someone as quiet and law-abiding as Naomi managed to get herself told off for shrieking in the main corridor. They were all given order marks. Nadge was actually given three, for 'endangering life and limb'. By the end of the first week after exams the weekly total had shot up from a respectable eight to an eyebrow-raising twenty-four.

'Jo, what *is* going on?' said Elizabeth, at the House meeting the following week. 'You've been doing so well! I was beginning to think we were really in with a chance

121

. . . I hope you're not going to go and blow it right at the last moment?'

'Absolutely not,' said Jo.

She went straight back to 1N and read them a lecture: it was greeted with hostility.

'Don't say you're starting on that again!'

'For goodness' *sake*!'

'Crawl back into your dustbin!'

'But you promised,' said Jo.

'Yes, and we've kept our promise. You can't deny it.' Barge and Bozzy, with the Bookends as back-up, cornered Jo in the playground during afternoon break.

'We've been good as *gold*,' said Bozzy. 'For positively *ages*.'

'There is a limit, you know. You don't want to push people too far.'

'It isn't natural, having to watch oneself the whole time.'

'I personally,' said Emma, 'am growing quite neurotic. You can't even *breathe* without wondering if she's going to leap out at you.'

'That's not fair!' Jo was indignant. She had kept to her side of the bargain just as well as them. 'I haven't leapt on anyone!'

'That's because there hasn't been any reason for you to leap on anyone. Nobody,' said Barge, 'has done anything that is leapable-on. As it were.'

'Except just for teeny-weeny little itsy-bitsy things that can't be helped.'

'Yes, like that incident on the bus when I just happened to tread backwards on to someone by mistake. And then my elbow kind of knocked into

122

someone's stupid eye. *Also* by mistake. And then this idiot went and tripped over my foot, which was just standing about on the floor same as feet always do. And then they had the nerve to say I was pushing and jostling. Honestly!' said Barge. 'I ask you! Am I *likely* to push and jostle?'

There was a discreet pause, then Emma said, 'Yes, actually. But that's not the point. The point is that that day when the Mouse and I went down the road we didn't *mean* to go into the Chinese takeaway. What we *meant* to do was go into the sandwich shop. But the sandwich shop has gone –'

'Gone!'

'Just a big hole –'

'A huge gaping gap –'

'Where the sandwich shop used to be –'

'And nobody told us.'

'Nobody!'

'So how were we to know?'

'The point *is*, you weren't meant to be out of school at all!' said Jo, exasperated. 'It didn't matter whether it was the sandwich shop or the takeaway, you WEREN'T MEANT TO BE THERE. If we carry on like this we'll stand no chance at all of winning the Cup.'

'Pardon me while I yawn,' said Bozzy.

'You really must guard against getting obsessed,' said Barge, who at the beginning of the year had been pretty obsessed herself. 'Competition is bad for the soul, and winning is *not* everything.'

'Not by any manner of means.'

'I would even venture so far as to suggest that it is positively *vulgar*.'

123

'You didn't always seem to think it vulgar,' said Jo. 'Last term, you said we'd got to beat Sutton or die in the attempt. That's what you *said*. When we were all writing our poems for the mag. –'

'That's right,' said Emma. 'Bring your poem into it. I thought that would come up, sooner or later.'

'Bragging is such bad manners. At least,' said Barge, 'that is what I have always been taught.'

Jo stamped her foot. 'I'm not bragging! I just don't want us to let people down by ruining our chances . . . I gave my word!'

'Who to?'

'To Elizabeth.'

'Oh. *Elizabeth*.' Barge nodded, heavily; the others followed suit. 'We all know about *Elizabeth*.'

'Some people,' said Emma, 'are rather overimpressed by Elizabeth.'

'She is only human, you know, the same as the rest of us.'

Jo's cheeks were so red, what with anger and what with embarrassment, her throat had gone so tight, her hands so clenched, that it seemed safer to turn on her heel and walk away.

'I'm warning you!' she choked. 'If there's any more of it –'

'What?'

'I shall put you on report!' cried Jo.

For the next day or so there was an uneasy truce. The Mouse got an order mark for cheeking a prefect, Bozzy got an order mark for leaving her *Junior Maths I* in the playground, where it got rained on and ruined, but no one actually misbehaved on purpose. (You couldn't

124

really count cheeking a prefect as misbehaving on purpose: some prefects almost *invited* you to cheek them. Even Jo accepted that.) On the other hand, there was a definite atmosphere. A definite feeling of anti-Jam – except that she had now reverted to being Bossyboots again.

She overheard Barge and Bozzy discussing the possible rounders team for the interhouse rally at the end of term:

'I *suppose* Bossyboots will be in it.'

'I suppose so.'

Pause.

'Jolly well serve her right if she wasn't!'

One Wednesday, when they should have been having Private Studies supervised by Pauline Marsh, Elizabeth stuck her head round the door and said, 'Jo, Pauline's been sent home with a sick headache. Can you manage to hold the fort, do you think, for a few minutes? I'll be with you just as soon as I can.'

Almost before the door had closed on Elizabeth there was a joyous cry of 'Hurroo!' and Nadge had gone leaping out of her desk and gibbering about the room like a monkey, uttering shrill cries and every now and again stopping to scratch, monkeylike, in her armptis.

Jo said, 'Nadge! Stop it!' But of course it was useless. Within seconds, half the class were capering up and down the aisles being monkeys.

'Have a nut, have a nut!' The Lollipop, well prepared as usual with a stock of food, held out a bag of salted peanuts. Nadge snatched at it and went loping off, on all fours, making little whimpering noises.

'*Stop it*!' cried Jo. She took up a stance behind Miss

125

Lloyd's desk, banging with her fist on the top. 'Everybody sit down!'

Needless to say, nobody did. If Nadge had done so, the rest would have followed; but Nadge had entered one of her manic phases. They came upon her from time to time, usually when she had been under some kind of stress, such as having to sit still for almost a week because of exams.

'Kibble kibble kibble,' chattered Nadge, jumping on top of Claire's desk.

'Get down off there!' shouted Jo.

Nadge made a rude gesture (a *very* rude gesture: the sort of gesture Tom sometimes made), leapt on to the windowsill, pranced along to the end of it and in one athletic bound went swinging across to the roof of the stationery cupboard, from which safe perch she proceeded to pelt Jo with salted peanuts.

'If you don't get down off there *immediately*,' yelled Jo, dodging a shower of peanuts, 'I shall put you on report!'

By way of reply, Nadge only chattered some more and lobbed another handful.

'Nadge! Nadge!' That was Jool, excitedly running out into the aisle. 'Have a banana!'

Nadge caught the banana in one hand as it came flying towards her. She did a little victory dance on top of the cupboard, stripped the banana, stuffed it into her mouth and carelessly tossed the skin down to Jo. The skin caught Jo slap in the face: it was clammy and horrible. At the same time, a peanut bounced off her forehead and an ominous splintering came from the roof of the stationery cupboard.

'Right!' screamed Jo. 'That's it! I warned you!'

She flung open the lid of Miss Lloyd's desk and clawed up the order mark book. At the back of the order mark book was a section where form captains or prefects, pushed to extremes, could place people on special report. It was hardly ever used; indeed the report section at the back of 1N's book was a complete blank. Jo didn't care. She was too angry to care. She snatched up a pen and jabbed it furiously on to the page.

NADIA FOSTER, she wrote, in big angry letters. She put the date, she put the time, and she signed it.

'There!' said Jo.

A sudden silence had come over the room. Jool retreated, nervously, to her desk. Nadge, with an air of unconcern, began the descent from the stationery cupboard. Barge took a long quivering breath.

'You shouldn't have done that,' she said.

Jo became conscious of fourteen pairs of eyes, all trained on her: Bozzy's, pale blue and bulging; Fij's, grave and reproachful; Gerry's cool, detached, superior; Emma's, blazing hatred; Melanie's, full of outrage; all of them, accusing.

'You shouldn't have done it,' repeated Barge.

The door opened and Elizabeth reappeared.

'Everything all right?' she said.

11

'Doing it to Nadge!'

'Of *all* people.'

Bad enough doing it to anyone. But to do it to *Nadge* –
1N were incensed. Even Fij was finding it difficult to
make excuses.

'You just don't *put* people on report. I mean . . . it's
just not something you *do*.'

'I warned her,' said Jo. Secretly she herself was feeling
rather shaken. 'I told her, if she didn't come down –'

'Yes, I know you *told* her. But people are always
telling people things. It doesn't necessarily mean they're
going to go ahead and *do* them. I have just never *known*
anyone be put on report. Except just once, but that was
years ago, a girl called Heidi Briggs, and she did
something *really* awful.'

'What?' said Jo. 'What did she do?'

'I can't remember, but it was something really bad,
like stealing or something.'

'And what –' Jo asked it as casually as she could –
'what happened to her?'

'She got chucked out,' said Fij. 'That's what happened
to her.'

Jo swallowed. No one would ever forgive her if Nadge
were to be chucked out. 'Jumping about on a stationery
cupboard isn't the same as stealing,' she said.

'Well, precisely,' said Fij. 'If someone were caught stealing I can imagine you *might* put them on report. But just for jumping on a *stationery* cupboard –'

Words, quite obviously, failed her. She gave Jo a look which shrivelled Jo's soul. Barge and Bozzy weren't speaking to her, nor were the Bookends, nor were Melanie and Ash, nor was the Lollipop. She didn't mind about any of them, but she did mind about Fij.

'Not even the Dictator ever did that to anyone,' said Fij.

Jo was moved, through sheer desperation, to defend herself. 'Nobody ever behaved like that with Gerry!'

Fij stopped, to consider the point. One thing about Fij, she was always scrupulously fair.

'That is true, I suppose, and I *do* see that it's difficult for you, what with Miss Lloyd not letting you give your badge in and Elizabeth going on about the House and everything, but to do it to Nadge was just so terrible.'

Jo hung her head. She was beginning to feel like a public executioner. How could she have done such a thing? To Nadge, of all people. Everyone knew that Nadge was excitable; she wouldn't be Nadge if she weren't. It was like Barge being overbearing and Bozzy being scatterbrained. They couldn't help it: they just were. Barge bullied, Bozzy flapped, and Nadge jumped around on the top of stationery cupboards. And now Jo had gone and put her on report.

She looked appealingly at Fij. 'They wouldn't chuck Nadge out,' she said. 'Not just for messing about.'

'Who knows?' said Fij. 'Last time she was in trouble, Miss Curtis said if she didn't start learning how to control herself she might have to be sent to a special school.'

'I didn't know that,' said Jo, miserably.

'No, well, you couldn't be expected to,' said Fij. 'That was in the Homestead; in our last term.'

'Well, but since she *has* controlled herself – I mean really, on the whole –'

'She's been really good, for her,' said Fij. 'Up until now.'

That made Jo feel guilty all over again; as if she were in some way to blame not only for getting Nadge into trouble but for causing her to have a break-out in the first place.

'What'll happen?' she said. 'She won't have to go to Miss Durndell, will she?'

'Mrs Stanley, probably. Then if Mrs Stanley thinks it's serious enough she'll send her to Miss Walters. But before then there's the tribunal.'

'*Tribunal*?' Jo stared at her, horrified. A tribunal sounded like law courts and judges and people being sentenced.

'Yes,' said Fij. 'You have to appear before all the House representatives and tell them what happened and why you put the person on report, and then the person can either plead guilty or not guilty, and the House has to decide what to do.'

Jo was chastened; she hadn't realized all that was involved. If she had known, would she still have put Nadge on report?

'Couldn't I just go and say it was a mistake?'

'You could,' said Fij, 'but they'd still want to know what happened. Once you've reported someone, that is *it*. You can't just wipe it out again and pretend you never did it.'

Wild thoughts rushed through Jo's head . . . she could lose the order mark book – tear the back page out of it –

'I could tear the back page out of it!'

'What?'

'The order mark book . . . I could tear the page out!'

'Mm. . . .' Fij sounded doubtfully encouraging. 'I s'ppose you *could*.'

'Well, who's to know?'

'They'd discover when the first page fell out, which is what it almost certainly *would* do.'

'But the first page is old!' The first page went right back to the start of the year, to last September. 1N had filled a great many pages with order marks since then. 'I could take the first page out as well!'

'You'd get into hideous trouble,' said Fij. 'That's tampering with the evidence, that is.'

Jo pulled a strand of hair into her mouth and chewed on it. Across the playground she could see Nadge practising catches with Lee Powell. They had an old cricket ball and were bouncing it off the wall at the back of the Science block. Nadge was going to make a really first-class wicket keeper one of these days – Elizabeth had said so. She was small and supple and incredibly fast. Suppose Miss Durndell chucked her out and she was sent to a school where they didn't play cricket?

'I think I'd better go and do it quickly,' said Jo. 'Before the bell goes.'

'That'll be an order mark,' said Fij, 'if anyone catches you.'

'I know, but if I don't do it now it'll be too late.'

Jo very nearly made it. She dodged round Wendy Armstrong, busy gossiping to a companion while on duty in the lower corridor, raced up the stairs, shot past the staff room, the door of which was closed, along the upper corridor, round the corner – and slap bang into Michelle Wandres.

'Jo Jameson!' snapped Michelle. 'What are you doing indoors during the lunch break?'

'I – er – um – wanted something,' said Jo.

'Wanted what?'

'Something from my – er – bag. *Desk*. Bag *in* desk. Book in bag. In desk,' babbled Jo.

Michelle's eyes narrowed. (They were pretty narrow to begin with.) 'Have you asked permission?'

'Er – no. That is –'

'That is what?'

'That is – no,' said Jo. 'Actually.'

Now Michelle's lips narrowed as well as her eyes. (They were even *narrower* to begin with. 'Old Michelle Mealy Mouth' was how Bozzy referred to her.)

'I am just about *sick* –' the words came out as a venomous hiss – 'of you lot in the First Year thinking you can take the law into your own hands and do whatever you please. There happen to be *rules* in this establishment, and you are expected to *keep* those rules. Everybody else has to. By what right,' snarled Michelle, lashing herself into a prefectorial fury, 'do you set yourselves above the rest of the school?'

Jo blinked.

'Well?'

'Er –' said Jo.

'Don't um and er and try to make excuses! That's all I ever hear from you people . . . *I didn't think, I didn't mean, I wasn't looking, I couldn't help it*. . . . Well, I've had enough of it! It's high time you were taught a lesson. Go in there –' Michelle pointed, dramatically, to 1N's form room. 'Fetch the order mark book and bring it to me.'

Perhaps, thought Jo, later, a braver soul would have ripped out the pages under cover of the desk lid. Jo didn't dare; and her last faint hope of being able to do it as she took the book back was shattered by the bell for the end of break, which rang as Michelle was angrily making her entry. Watching her, Jo found it difficult to believe that scarcely an hour ago she had been making an angry entry of her own, at the other end of the book. How *could* she have lost her temper like that, all because Nadge was having a moment of madness?

There might still have been time to carry out her sabotage, but Miss Lloyd arrived, in her usual cloud of gorgeous perfume, before Michelle had finished signing her name.

'Jo! What's this?' she said. 'An order mark?' She took the book from Michelle and twitched an eyebrow. 'Not what I expect from you,' she said.

From somewhere behind her, Jo heard a suppressed snigger. She turned, and saw the Lollipop. Her heart sank: the news would be all round the class in no time.

It was. By the following morning everyone knew that Bossyboots (otherwise known as Mrs Thatcher, Goody Two-Shoes, St Jam-ima), had been given an order mark.

'Her that thinks herself so bleeding wonderful!'

'*Now* let her have a go at the rest of us.'

It wasn't really fair, since it was the first order mark Jo had had all term, but she could understand that they felt exultant; she would probably have felt the same, in their place.

On Friday, the order mark books were handed in and the weekly totals added up. Soon, in fact almost at any moment, Kay was going to discover what was lurking at the back. Jo spent the whole afternoon in a state of sick apprehension. Nadge, on the other hand, seemed her usual carefree self. They had double Art after lunch on a Friday. Mrs Halley, the Art mistress, never kept very strict discipline: Nadge giggled and joked and fooled around exactly the same as she always did. Was she really not worried or was it an act of bravado?

Jo was just beginning to cherish a tiny little faint wisp of hope that maybe nobody ever bothered looking at the back page of an order mark book (since almost nothing was ever written there), when the door of the Art Studio opened and one of the prefects looked round. Philippa Drew; a mate of Mealy Mouth and very nearly as putrid. She said, 'Terribly sorry to interrupt, but could I possibly have a quick word with Jo Jameson and Nadia Foster?'

Jo's blood went draining out of her veins and collecting in a big cold puddle in the pit of her stomach. As she walked to the door after Nadge (how could Nadge *bounce* like that?) she felt the eyes of everyone in the class following them.

'OK,' said Philippa. 'You know what it's about. We were going to leave it till the normal weekly meeting, but then we thought, as it's rather serious, we'd better call a special session just to deal with it. We've arranged it for first break on Monday, in the Senior Library. Kay said please to make sure you both turn up and please to make sure that you're punctual.'

Jo tried hard to catch Nadge's eye as they went back

into the studio, but Nadge didn't give her the chance. She went prancing ahead of Jo through the door, irrepressible as ever.

'Hey, Mrs Halley, I just had an idea for something I'd like to paint!'

'What's that?' said Mrs Halley, always keen to encourage the nonartists amongst them.

'Black cat in the dark with its eyes closed!' said Nadge.

Everyone laughed except Jo.

Down in the cloakroom at the end of afternoon school a girl from Roper's sidled up to Jo, and keeping a wary eye on the rest of 1N whispered, 'I don't blame you, putting Nadia Foster on report. It was about time someone did. They've *never* been able to control her. I don't think she's fit to be at an ordinary school. P'raps now they'll do something about it.'

Jo was flabbergasted. How did this horrible Roperite know about Nadge being on report? And who was she, anyway?

'Old Droopy Drawers,' said Fij. 'What's she want?'

Jo jumped, guiltily. 'Oh! N-nothing much.' She felt as if she had been caught fraternizing with the enemy. There were times when one would almost rather *not* have people offer their support if they were going to gloat and be self-righteous. 'Why's she called Droopy Drawers?'

'Because she's droopy and so are her drawers. She used to be in the Homestead with us. We were most incredibly grateful,' said Fij, 'when she was put into Roper's. All the rubbish is put into Roper's. Nellie's gets the cream, then Sutton, then York. Roper's,' said Fij, 'is just crammed full of nobodies.'

135

It did seem to be true. Now she came to think about it, Jo couldn't recall the name of one single Roperite.

'What did she want,' said Fij, 'anyway? What was she doing here, on our patch?'

Jo muttered, 'She'd heard about Nadge.'

'*Oh.*' Fij instantly busied herself taking her blazer off its peg, fussily putting it on and doing it up, then promptly undoing it again, then stooping to fiddle with the strap on her sandals. 'Hey, Barge!' she yelled, as she straightened up. 'Wait for us!'

Fij shot up the cloakroom stairs after Barge and Bozzy, leaving Jo on her own. Sadly, Jo picked up her bag and followed them out. There was no point in rushing to catch them up: they were making it all too obvious that they didn't want her.

She found herself walking up Shapcott Road in company with Claire. Claire looked at the other three, who were marching ahead. 'Are they mad at you?' she said.

Jo nodded, not trusting herself to speak.

'I shouldn't let it bother you,' said Claire. 'They were mad at me, that one time . . . d'you remember? All because I wouldn't play their idiotic game of netball?' She giggled. 'They sent me to Coventry and I didn't even know till it was all over and you told me about it!'

Jo managed a faint smile. She supposed it had been quite funny, people like Barge and Bozzy ostentatiously not talking and Claire totally failing to notice.

'They can't help it,' said Claire. 'In some ways they're terribly childish. They still seem to think that school is the most important thing in their lives.'

Well, but it *was*, thought Jo. It mightn't be for Claire,

rushing off to do her ballet every day, but it was for ordinary, normal people. And unlike Claire, Jo *noticed* when the class weren't talking.

'Do you want to come and watch my ballet lesson?' said Claire. 'I expect Miss Lintott might let you if I ask.'

Jo shook her head. 'It's all right, thank you. I've got to get home for the Youth Club.'

She said she had to get home for the Youth Club, but when the time came she really wondered whether she wanted to go. Nadge would be there, and how could she possibly face her?

'It's half-past six,' said Mrs Jameson. 'Shouldn't you be getting ready?'

'If I'm going.'

'What do you mean, if you're going? What's come over you all of a sudden? I thought you liked the Youth Club?'

Jo shrugged.

'I was under the impression,' said Mrs Jameson, slyly, 'that a certain young gentleman by the name of Robbie awaited your presence . . .'

Robbie! She had forgotten about Robbie. He would be expecting her. She decided that she would go upstairs and get dressed – red tights, with baggy black T-shirt and white baseball boots – and wait to see what happened. If Matty called for her the same as usual, she would go; if Matty didn't call then she would stay home and pretend to have a headache.

She couldn't decide whether she was relieved or not when her mother called up the stairs that Matty had arrived. She was relieved that they were still on speaking terms, but it didn't do anything to quell her apprehensions: what was she going to say to Nadge?

As it happened, she didn't have to say anything to Nadge because Nadge didn't say anything to Jo. It wasn't so much that she deliberately avoided her as that she made sure their paths didn't cross. Or maybe it was Jo who made sure. Or maybe they both did. Jo stood on one side of the room with Robbie, and Matty's brother Miles, and one or two others who liked peace and quiet, while Nadge stayed on the other side, surrounded as always by a horde, including, naturally, Tom.

Halfway through the evening Mrs Barlow announced that they were going to do impersonations. Everyone liked that. Not everyone was brave enough to join in – Miles, for instance, was far too shy – but everyone enjoyed trying to guess who the others were impersonating.

Tom did his celebrated takeoff of Fij's hero, Bobby-Jo. (It wasn't very good. The only reason people recognized it was that Tom kept saying 'Jeepers creepers!', which was Bobby-Jo's catchphrase.) Nadge did Mrs Barlow, running her fingers through her hair and saying distractedly, 'All *right*, everybody! *Now* –' Mrs Barlow laughed louder than anyone.

Matty and Jool did the Two Eclairs (a Black singing duo), Robbie did a famous footballer that Jo had never heard of and that nobody could guess. Robbie wasn't an extrovert like Tom and Nadge, but he was always willing to give it a go.

When it was Jo's turn she did Bo Peep singing 'Eeny Meeny Macaraca', which was what she sang on her latest single. Of course it wasn't the same without the Bad Boys as backing, but still she would have thought people could have guessed. Instead, when Mrs Barlow said, 'All right, everybody! Who was that?' Tom's voice bellowed, 'Margaret Thatcher!' and they all fell about.

'Why did they say Mrs Thatcher?' said Robbie, puzzled, as he and Jo stood together afterwards drinking Coke.

''Cause they're idiots!' said Jo. 'It's their stupid idea of a joke.' She sucked vigorously at the straw in her Coke bottle. The drink came whizzing up in a great gush and almost choked her. After Robbie had kindly (if somewhat ineffectually) walloped her on the back, and Coke bubbles had stopped sizzling in her nose, Jo said, 'I wish I could go to a mixed school. All girls is *horrible*.'

'So's all boys,' said Robbie, 'sometimes.'

'I bet it's not as horrible as all girls! Girls are cats.'

Robbie said, 'I like cats.'

'You wouldn't like this lot!'

'I don't expect you'd like our lot, either,' said Robbie.

'I wouldn't if they were all like Tom.' Jo stared malevolently across the room at her brother, who was doing some kind of impersonation (*her*? Was it supposed to be *her*?) at which everyone was laughing. 'But they're not all like Tom,' she said, 'are they?'

'Some are worse than Tom. Tom's OK. We've got some right yobs in some years.'

'What kinds of yobs?'

'Yobs that go round beating people up.'

Jo's eyes widened. 'Really beating people up?'

'They pulled a knife on one boy last term,' said Robbie. 'Your lot aren't as bad as that.'

They weren't, of course. Not even Jo could pretend that calling people names and not talking to them was as bad as attacking them with knives; but that still didn't make the prospect of Monday morning any easier to bear.

'Cheer up,' said Robbie. 'It's nearly the end of term – and don't forget,' he said, 'I'm coming to see you play rounders.'

12

'When you say, *jumped on the stationery cupboard –*' Kay paused, to let the words sink in. Someone (Katy Wells?) sniggered. Someone else (Michelle Wandres?) snapped, 'This is no laughing matter!'

'Precisely. Jumping on a stationery cupboard is no cause for hilarity. It's exceedingly foolish, for one thing; for another it could be said to constitute damage to school property.'

'An act of ill-disciplined vandalism,' said Michelle.

'Yes, and that too,' agreed Kay. 'So perhaps you could explain –' she turned back to Jo – 'exactly in what manner and why Nadia jumped on to the stationery cupboard?'

'Um – yes. Well –' Jo cast an agonized glance in Nadge's direction, but Nadge was doing complicated things with her fingers, interlacing them and crossing them one over another until they looked to be inextricably tangled. She seemed far more interested in her fingers than in the tribunal.

'Yes?' said Kay. She said it quite kindly. 'Take your time; we're not rushing you.'

'Yes, well, the thing is,' said Jo, 'I expect what it was, I expect there was something up there, probably, that had got there my mistake, like a rubber or a – a stray hedgehog, or something, and it couldn't get down, and what happened was that Nadge climbed up to get it and I didn't realize at the time that that was what she was doing, but it probably was what she was doing, I should think,' said Jo.

There was a silence.

'I see,' said Kay. She looked penetratingly at Jo for a few seconds, then slowly transferred her gaze to Nadge, who was still busy weaving her fingers together. '*Was* that what you were doing, Nadia?'

'Not really,' said Nadge.

'You mean –' the corners of Kay's mouth twitched ever so slightly – 'there wasn't any stray hedgehog on top of the stationery cupboard?'

'Didn't see one,' said Nadge.

'No stray elephants? Chipmunks? Hippopotamuses? Armadillos?'

Nadge shook her head.

'So what, if I may ask, were you *doing* on the stationery cupboard?'

'I was dancing,' said Nadge.

'Dancing; on top of the stationery cupboard. You really think,' said Kay, 'that the top of a stationery cupboard is the right place for dancing?'

Nadge shrugged, and concentrated on her fingers.

'Well, I'll tell you what,' said Kay, 'I certainly don't. And looking at your record – your *personal* record – of order marks for this term, I have to say that I am not very impressed. I should hardly call it giving support to your form captain, would you?'

Nadge said nothing; Jo squirmed.

'There has just been altogether too much of this kind of thing from you, Nadia; I honestly don't know whether

142

we can deal with it ourselves. It may be a case for special treatment. I'm going to put it to the vote: do we just dish out order marks, or do we ask Mrs Stanley to intervene?'

Nadge was popular; but she also had a reputation for being trouble. When the voting papers were handed in and the votes counted, Kay announced that the House had decided, by 14–6, that Nadge should be sent to Mrs Stanley. Jo guessed that twelve of those fourteen votes would almost certainly be from the prefects. The other two, she bet, were from Martha Prince and Katy Wells. They would be only too happy to see a First Year in hot water – and it was all Jo's fault!

'Don't look so glum,' said Elizabeth, as Nadge was marched out, like a prisoner under armed guard, to see Mrs Stanley. 'You can't win 'em all – and Nadia has always been a maniac.'

She hadn't been a maniac when Gerry was in charge. She had had her moments, but nothing as batty as dancing on top of the stationery cupboard.

'Jo!' Wendy Armstrong had come back from escorting Nadge. She beckoned to Jo across the room. 'Mrs Stanley said could she have a quick word with you as well?'

'M-me?' said Jo.

'Yes, you! Come along!'

Jo walked, leaden-footed, up the corridor with Wendy to Mrs Stanley's room.

'There you are.' Wendy pointed to a chair outside. 'Take a seat, she'll call you when she's ready.'

Mrs Stanley was House head mistress; she also taught Maths. In spite of Jo being a mathematical moron, she and Mrs Stanley actually understood each other quite

143

well. For all that, Jo would rather not have been dumped outside her room and told to wait. It felt very exposed, sitting in the corridor: it also felt ominous. Why did Mrs Stanley want to see her as well as Nadge? Was it because she was going to recommend to Miss Durndell that Nadge be thrown out, and she wanted to tell Jo before she told anyone else?

The bell rang for the end of break and people began to stream in from the playground. Fortunately, Mrs Stanley's office was not on direct route to 1N's form room so Jo was spared the ignominy of being seen by any of her formmates. It was bad enough being stared at by various members of 1S as they walked past, especially by Lee Powell. Lee was aggressive at the best of times. If she knew that Nadge was inside, possibly being expelled, she would bear grudges from now until the end of time.

Everybody would bear grudges. She would almost rather be expelled herself. At least then she would be able to make a fresh start at a new school with new people instead of dragging out a miserable existence, shunned and reviled and generally spat upon, here at Peter's.

At last, when the corridor was empty (which would mean being late for Singing, which would mean explaining) the door of Mrs Stanley's room opened and Nadge came out. She didn't look at Jo but went running off up the stairs – not before Jo had noticed, however, that her eyes were red and that in one hand she clutched a crumpled handkerchief. *Nadge*? *Crying*? It confirmed all Jo's worst fears.

She wobbled upright on trembling legs as Mrs Stanley put her head round the door and said, 'Jo? Come in!'

144

Mrs Stanley didn't *sound* like someone who has just arranged for a person to be expelled; she sounded quite cheerful. Maybe that was because she left the actual expelling for Miss Durndell to handle. Miss Durndell was always rather grim; she probably enjoyed expelling people.

'All right, Jo!' Mrs Stanley smiled, reassuringly. 'There's no need to look scared! I only wanted to tell you how well I think you've coped this term.'

How well? Jo blinked.

'It can't have been easy for you, following in Gerry's footsteps – especially as I suspect there was an element of rebellion involved. Am I right? Yes!' (as Jo's cheeks flared a giveaway red) 'I thought there was. I know that lot only too well. You've got some real live wires there – and Nadia, of course, is more than just a live wire, she's your actual electric shocker! I'm not surprised you had to put her on report; it was bound to happen one of these days. Don't count it against yourself that you couldn't tame Nadia. Nobody can – and I'm afraid that even includes me.'

But Mrs Stanley had reduced Nadge to tears! She must have threatened her with something pretty dire.

'Hopefully as she grows up she'll grow out of her madcapness; all we can do in the meantime is try to contain her as best we can. You're still looking bothered! What's the problem?'

'Will she have to go to Miss Durndell?' said Jo.

'Not on this occasion. I have warned her, however, that if it happens again . . . which I have no doubt it will; one has to be realistic. But if she can manage to scrape through the rest of this term and at least the beginning of next without getting into trouble, I shall count it a victory!'

Jo's heart lifted. So Nadge wasn't being expelled after all! Things might still be bad, but they could have been a whole lot worse. At least now she could concentrate on enjoying what was left of the term. It wasn't as if *every*body had stopped speaking to her. Fij was still speaking; and Claire, and Matty, and Jool. And maybe, just maybe, if she managed to distinguish herself in the interhouse rounders on Saturday they would forget what she had done to Nadge. Whether Nadge would forget was, of course, another matter.

Jo collected her books from the form room, where some Third Years were having English with Miss Lloyd, and hurried off to the Music Studio, from which could be heard the hideous and repellent sound of 1N singing. As she came through the door all eyes swivelled in her direction. Mouths opened and shut; some mouths, such as Barge's, opened wider than others. Barge had a voice like an out-of-tune foghorn, but that didn't stop her singing at the top of her voice.

Bozzy was busy warbling on one side of her, Fij fluting on the other. From the row behind came the Bookends' lusty bellow – the Bookends enjoyed singing, even though they were almost totally tone deaf – and from the row behind that a high-pitched squeaking and groaning which could either be loose floorboards or Melanie and Ash; there wasn't really any way of telling one from the other. Over the whole rose the Lollipop's clear soprano, supported by Matty's contralto and Claire's undistinguished but at least musical tones. They were the only three who had any pretensions to being able to sing.

Jo scuttled to her place beside Fij, making herself as inconspicuous as possible. Nadge, she couldn't help noticing, was not there.

'Jo, you're late!' Mrs Elliott brought the song to a close. (Barge, two bars behind everyone else, went on singing.) 'I know it's only *music*, and not wondrous modern technology, but I do expect punctuality all the same.'

'I've been with Mrs Stanley,' muttered Jo; and heard a sharp intake of breath from Barge and Bozzy, further along the row.

At that moment Nadge burst into the room. Her face was scrunched into a puckish beam, all trace of tears completely gone.

'Sorry I'm late; I've been being told off.'

Another sharp intake. All the eyes moved anxiously to Nadge. Mrs Elliott played a quick arpeggio.

'Not to worry, Nadia, we've had no call for basses today.'

Nadge, last week, had had everyone in fits by singing in a deep, gravelly growl. Fortunately Mrs Elliott didn't believe in giving people order marks; she had simply said, 'Carry on like that, my dear, and you'll soon have no voice left at all – which come to think of it might be a blessed relief. You're not really what could be called musical, are you?'

With a cheeky grin Nadge dashed off to join Jool and Matty in the back row. It was hard to believe that only a few minutes ago she had emerged in tears from her talk with Mrs Stanley. But she *had* been in tears, and it was Jo who had caused it. Jo wished there were some way she could make it up to her. There was only one way she could think of and that was to play her very, very best on Saturday. If 1N were to beat not only the other First Years but the Seconds and Thirds as well, and it was all, or very largely, thanks to Jo, even Nadge might forgive her.

That evening, Jo said carelessly to Tom, 'Fancy a game in the garden?'

'What sort of game?'

It wasn't any use saying rounders: rounders was a girl's game.

'Baseball?' said Jo.

Tom looked at her, knowingly. 'You just want to practise for this thing on Saturday,' he said.

Damn! Now he wouldn't do it. Tom could be really pig-headed if he thought you wanted something from him.

'All right. If you don't feel like it,' said Jo.

'Hang about! Who said I didn't feel like it? Did *I* say I didn't feel like it? Don't you go getting on your high horse with me, Squit Face! Apologize, or I won't come.'

'You mean you will if I do?' said Jo.

'I might. Just for half an hour.'

'I apologize.'

'Come on, then!'

It was fun, playing with Tom – when he felt like playing. This evening he obviously did because he stayed out there in the garden until almost eight o'clock, when 'Spaceball', one of his favourite programmes, was on television. To Jo's surprise and secret gratification (it wasn't often that Tom allowed himself to show any interest in her affairs) he suggested again, the following night, that they went out there.

'Don't forget,' he said, 'I'll be coming along to watch you Saturday.'

'*You* will?' said Jo.

Tom bristled. 'I suppose I can if I want?'

Of course, she suddenly twigged: he was coming to watch Nadge. But naturally he couldn't *say* he was coming to watch Nadge. That would be a sign of weakness. He had to pretend that he was coming to watch Jo, purely out of a sense of duty, because of her being his sister. (But when had he ever cared two straws before?)

'Me and Robbie,' he said. 'We're going to wear our supporters' shirts.'

'Your *what*?'

'Supporters' shirts . . . we've had them done specially. They've got UP NELLIE'S on the front and DOWN WITH EVERYBODY ELSE on the back.'

'Cripes,' said Jo. She wondered nervously how Elizabeth would feel. She hoped she wouldn't say that it was warlike and 'not good sportsmanship'.

'And we're bringing a rattle,' said Tom, 'and a hooter. So you'd better be good. It's the only reason I'm wasting my time on you. . . . We don't want to be made to look stupid.'

'No, I see,' said Jo, prepared to be humble if it achieved her object.

Her object was to hit more rounders than anyone else so that Nadge would come up to her and say 'It's all thanks to you that we won!' and everybody would congratulate her and forget that they weren't on speaking terms.

By Thursday evening Jo was cracking every ball Tom

149

flung at her to the garden fence and even beyond. Next door (not Matty's side, the other) was starting to complain, but it didn't matter: Jo felt ready for anything. If she could hit Tom all over the place she could certainly deal with the First and Second Years, and maybe even the Third as well. They might be taller than Tom but they weren't anywhere near as aggressive.

She gave her white shorts and T-shirt to her mother, to be washed ready for Friday, and even cleaned her trainers, which were covered in grass stains from cricket.

'This is obviously a highly important occasion,' said Mrs Jameson. (She wasn't used to the sight of Jo cleaning anything.)

'Yes, it is,' said Jo, vigorously scrubbing. 'It's almost more important than anything else – well, apart from exams, of course,' she added, virtuously.

'Have you had your results yet?'

'Not yet,' said Jo. Exam results weren't out until next week; she would worry about them when the time came. For the moment she was concentrating all her energies on Saturday.

Everyone, even people like Pru, who hated all forms of sport, and Melanie, who affected to despise it, took an interest in the interhouse rounders.

'Is your sister coming?' said Jo, as she and Fij walked up Shapcott Road together on Friday evening.

'My sister?' said Fij. She sounded for some reason startled by the question.

'You know!' said Jo. 'That person called Jacqueline Jarvis that just happens to live in the same house as you?'

'Oh. Yes,' said Fij. She gave a nervous titter. 'Jacky.'

'*That's* right,' said Jo. '*Jacky*.' Jacky was ten, and still

150

in the Homestead. 'I knew you'd remember who she was if you thought about it long enough.'

Fij tittered again, a bit unconvincingly.

'So is she coming?' said Jo.

'Coming?' said Fij.

'Tomorrow,' said Jo.

'Ah. Tomorrow,' said Fij. She seemed uncomfortable; Jo couldn't think why. Little sisters *did* come – so did big brothers.

'Tom's threatened to turn up,' said Jo, 'wearing his supporters' shirt!'

Fij's pale cheeks had grown suddenly and rather hectically pink. Barge, walking a few paces ahead with Bozzy, cast a withering glance over her shoulder. 'I can't imagine what he wants to come for.'

'Well – you know!' Jo giggled. 'To watch me, he *says*. What he really means is watch Nadge.'

'So long as it is what he really means . . . one wouldn't want him to be disappointed.'

There was a pause; then in a tight little voice, Jo said: 'Why should he be disappointed?'

'If he thought he was going to watch you.' Barge flung it backwards into the air, not bothering even to turn her head.

'What does she mean?' said Jo, looking at Fij. Fij shook her head; her cheeks by now were bright scarlet.

Barge stopped, abruptly, and swung round to face them. Bozzy, skittering to a halt a few paces further on, came scuttling back sideways like a crab, anxious not to miss out.

'You surely don't suppose,' said Barge, 'you *surely* do not *suppose* that you are in the team?'

151

Jo's cheeks fired up as bright as Fij's.

'The nerve of it!' marvelled Barge. 'She puts someone on report and then expects them to include her in their rounders team! Did you ever –' she appealed to Bozzy – 'hear the like?'

'Never,' said Bozzy.

'Extra*ord*inary,' said Barge. 'Some people have a mighty high opinion of themselves!'

'Jo is one of our strongest players,' muttered Fij.

'She might be one of our strongest players, but she is not indispensable.'

'Winning isn't everything,' said Bozzy.

'It certainly is *not*,' agreed Barge.

'There is such a thing as being a good loser.'

'Precisely.'

Even in the depths of her stunned humiliation, Jo couldn't help wondering what Barge and Bozzy knew about being good losers. Barge and Bozzy couldn't *bear* losing. As Barge had once said, 'I don't see any point in playing if you don't play to win.'

Fij looked worriedly at Jo. 'Has Nadge said anything to you?'

'She has to us,' said Barge.

'She said, "Don't forget to be here by nine o'clock",' boasted Bozzy.

'So if she hasn't said it to you –'

Nadge hadn't said anything to Jo; she hadn't spoken since the incident of the cupboard. Jo had simply taken it for granted that she would still be playing. Only now, when she was forced to stop and think about it, did she see that she was probably the very *last* person Nadge would want on her team.

152

'Really!' said Barge.

Bozzy sniffed.

'The conceit of some people!'

Barge and Bozzy wheeled round and stalked off again, arm in arm, exuding self-righteousness.

'I'm ever so sorry,' said Fij, miserably.

'It's all right,' said Jo. You had to say it was all right, even if it wasn't. Even if you felt like rushing to the nearest dark hole and burying yourself.

'We usually discuss things,' said Fij. 'I mean . . . me being vice-captain, she usually talks it over with me. But this time she didn't.'

They both knew the reason. It was because Fij was Jo's friend and it might have been embarrassing.

'It's all right,' said Jo, again. 'It really doesn't matter.'

'But I just don't know who she's going to put in your place.'

All term the rounders team had been:

Pitcher	. . . . . .	Barge
Backstop	. . . . . .	Nadge
1st Post	. . . . . .	Bozzy
2nd Post	. . . . . .	Emma
3rd Post	. . . . . .	Mouse
4th Post	. . . . . .	Jo
1st Deep	. . . . . .	Fij
2nd Deep	. . . . . .	Matty
3rd Deep	. . . . . .	Gerry

Bravely, Jo said: 'I expect she'll ask Lol; Lol's a lot better than people think. Just because she's fat she gets overlooked. It's probably a good thing, really, giving someone else a chance.'

'Not in the interhouse tournament,' said Fij. 'We may beat Roper and York, but we'll never beat Sutton; not without you.'

13

Jo didn't go to the Youth Club that evening. How could she possibly face Robbie? *Or* Tom? Tom would be furious, after all the hard work he had put in. He would say it had been nothing but a waste of time – which, of course, it had.

'I've got a headache,' yelled Jo, when Mrs Jameson called up the stairs that Matty was here. 'Tell her I'm not coming.'

By the next morning she really had a headache: that was because she had spent half the night lying awake being miserable. Tom came hammering on her bedroom door at half-past eight shouting at her to 'Get up, you lazy beast! You'll be late!'

Late for what? wondered Jo. She didn't think she could bear to go and watch the Lollipop (or whoever it was) playing instead of her.

'Are you awake?' Tom opened the door and shoved his head round. He was wearing his supporters' T-shirt, sky blue (for Nelligan) with UP NELLIE'S in large white stick-on letters. 'The first match is at nine o'clock.'

Jo rolled over and buried her head in the pillow. She was surprised that Nadge hadn't told him – 'Your sister isn't playing. She put me on report and got me into trouble so I've chucked her out of the team.' She wished in a way that she had – it would spare Jo having to do it –

but Nadge wasn't like that. She never gossiped about people. She was never spiteful or picky. She might chuck Jo out the team, but she wouldn't go round telling people about it.

'What are you *doing*?' bawled Tom, pushing at Jo and trying to turn her over.

'Leave me alone!' Jo pulled the duvet round her head. 'I feel sick.'

'You can't feel sick, you've got to play rounders!' Tom grabbed at the duvet and did his best to haul it off. Jo did her best to hang on. 'Get up!' roared Tom.

'What's the matter? What's going on?' Mrs Jameson had come into the room, alerted by the sounds of struggle. 'Tom, what are you doing? Jo, why aren't you up? I thought you had to be in by nine o'clock?'

'She has,' said Tom. 'She's *lazy*!'

'I feel sick.' Jo flipped over on to her back, doing her best to look pale and suffering. Mrs Jameson laid a hand on her forehead.

'You haven't got a temperature. I expect it's just nerves. You'll feel better once you're up and you've got some breakfast inside you. But you'd better hurry if you want your dad to give you a lift – he's leaving in fifteen minutes.'

'I'll go and marge your toast!'

Tom went galloping off down the stairs.

'That makes a nice change,' said Mrs Jameson. 'He's trying to be helpful for once!'

Jo could have wished – for once – that he wasn't. She climbed disconsolately out of bed and into her jeans and sweatshirt. Downstairs, Tom had prepared her toast – 'I put on oceans of honey! Gives you energy' – Mrs

Jameson had neatly folded her clean T-shirt and shorts and put them in a carrier along with her trainers, Mr Jameson was waiting, car keys in hand.

'Ten minutes,' he said. 'I'll give you ten minutes.'

Jo spun it out as long as she could, but not even she could make three pieces of toast and a glass of orange juice last more than ten minutes.

'Step on the gas!' cried Tom, hustling Jo into the car.

'I'm not exceeding the speed limit just for a game of rounders,' said Mr Jameson

'It's not just a game of rounders, it's UP NELLIE'S and DOWN WITH EVERYBODY ELSE!' Tom picked up his hooter and blew it. 'This is war, man!'

Mr Jameson shook his head. 'When I was at school we said it was the playing that mattered, not the winning.'

'Dad, that was yonks ago,' said Tom. 'Things have changed since then. We're not playing tiddlywinks, this is the real thing. If Nellie's don't win, after all the hours I've spent coaching this person –'

What? though Jo, listlessly staring out of the window. What would he do, if Nellie's didn't win?

'– I'll be jolly disgusted!' said Tom.

The town hall clock was striking the hour as the car pulled up outside the main gates of Peter's.

'Out you get,' said Mr Jameson. 'Have a good time. Win if that's what you want – but don't go throwing any bombs.'

'Dad's such an old woman,' said Tom.

Jo couldn't even summon up the energy to berate him for sexism.

They joined the trail of people walking towards the side entrance which led to the back of the school and the

157

playing field. Tom had just opened his mouth to say, 'Oughtn't you to b –' when there was a loud screech of 'JAM!' and Nadge appeared, winkling her way through the crowd.

'Jam! Come quick!' cried Nadge. 'We're starting!'

Jo wasn't given the chance to ask any questions. She found herself dragged at full pelt, bumping and banging, through a tangle of arms and legs, through the side gate, down the steps and into the cloakroom.

'Hurry, hurry!' urged Nadge. She tore Jo's carrier bag from her, tipped out the contents and began pulling at the laces on her trainers. Crazy thoughts raced through Jo's head. The Lollipop had fallen under a bus – Melanie had broken her ankle – Ash had got the measles – 'I wondered where you were,' said Nadge. She thrust Jo's T-shirt at her. 'I was getting really worried. Then Fij told me you didn't think you were still in the team.'

'B-Barge told me,' stammered Jo.

'You don't want to take any notice of anything Barge ever says!'

Jo blushed. 'I thought you were mad at me for getting you into trouble.'

'What trouble?' Nadge held out Jo's shorts. 'Oh, *that* trouble. That wasn't anything. I've been in far worse trouble. We'll *both* be in far worse trouble than that if you don't get a move on. Elizabeth said we could have five minutes and no more . . . are you ready?'

Together, Jo and Nadge went racing across to the field. A great cheer went up as they arrived. The people who were cheering were 1N and their supporters, including Tom and Robbie in their supporters' shirts, blowing their hooter and waving their rattle.

'Thank goodness you made it,' said Bozzy.

'Where on earth were you?' said Barge. 'We thought you weren't coming.'

Fij looked across at Jo and smiled, rather nervously. Jo grinned. Whoever took any notice of anything Barge ever said?

By the end of the first round, 1N had comfortably thrashed both York and Roper and even romped home against Sutton. Jo had covered herself in honour and glory and been loudly cheered by all the Nellie's supporters standing on the touchlines. (She had heard Tom's rattle and hooter and raucous bellowings of 'Up the Nellie's!' every time she hit a rounder, but she had been too flushed with success to be embarrassed.)

Having seen off all the opposition meant that 1N were top of their junior section and moved on to play the other junior section winners, who were 2S and 3N. The finalists in the senior section were 4S, 5S and 6N. As expected, York and Roper had been completely wiped out.

'That's twenty points for coming top of our section and ten more for every other game we manage to win,' exulted Barge, busy sucking orange slices during the break. 'Of course we shan't beat the Third Years, but they are Nellie's anyway, and we shall *certainly* smash the Second Years to a pulp.'

'Winning isn't everything,' murmured Fij, catching Jo's eye over the top of her Coke bottle.

'I *beg* your pardon?' Barge drew herself up, stiff and straight with outrage. 'In the circumstances, that remark might *al*most qualify as treason.'

Barge was really quite funny in her own way. The pity of it was, she didn't realize it.

If 1N weren't quite able to manage any smashing, they did quite respectably beat 2S by ten rounders to eight, and that, as Barge said, was not to be sneezed at, even if the Third Year rather trampled on them – 'Which is hardly surprising when you consider how huge they are, and anyway it's the House that matters, not personal glory. And I think we can safely say that as a *House* we have come out on top. And since Jammy hit more rounders than anyone else in our year,' concluded Barge, cosily, 'I think we can also say that even as a form we are not without honour. At any rate we've wiped the silly smirks off *some* people's faces.'

Katy Wells, who just happened to be passing as the remark was flung out, turned and snapped, 'If you're by any chance referring to us, Barge Laing, you'd better wait till the final order marks are added up . . . you might find yourself laughing on the other side of your face.'

'Whatever that means,' said Barge. She gave a short, scornful bark. 'Such tiny minds those Second Years have! Order marks or not, I should say that after today we shall almost certainly have won the Cup.'

The scoreboard looked good, there was no denying it. The final figures were:

Nellie's	 140
Sutton	 90
York	 30
Roper	 10

'Pretty conclusive, I think you will agree,' purred Barge.

'If it weren't for exam results,' said Bozzy, with a shudder, 'I could almost be quite happy.'

School broke up on Tuesday: exam results were given out on Monday. Bozzy, as she had glumly predicted, came bottom of almost everything (but not *quite* everything: in Geography she only came fourth from bottom, and in Biology only sixth, which caused Barge to thump her on the back and various other people to look at her in wonderment. It lifted her gloom considerably).

Gerry, as always, vied for top places with either Pru or Naomi.

'So boringly predictable,' sighed Barge.

There was only one major upset, and that was in English. It was Miss Lloyd who read out the results. Miss Lloyd had a habit – welcome to those such as Bozzy, who liked to get the bad news over with; not so welcome to Gerry & Co., who had to sit and sweat – of reading from the bottom up.

'Chloë Boswood,' read Miss Lloyd, '19 per cent.'

Nineteen? thought Jo. How could anyone possibly get nineteen for English? (Jo herself had admittedly got twenty for Maths, but Maths was different. Maths was *impossible*. In all other subjects that counted – that is to say, all the ones that parents got fussed over – she had as usual come somewhere in the middle.)

Miss Lloyd worked her way briskly up the list:

'Ashley Wilkerson, 25
Nadia Foster, 32
Laurel Bustamente, 40

Julie-Ann Gillon, 48
Sally Hutchins, 54
Emma Gilmore, 59
Margery Laing and Matty McShane, 61
Naomi Adams, 68
Felicity Jarvis, 70
Claire Kramer, 76
Prunella Frank, 77 –'

It was at this point that Fij pressed a finger into Jo's ribs and Jo's heart started hammering.

'Geraldine Stubbs, 80,' read Miss Lloyd,

'Joanne Jameson, 82.'

There was a rush as of hot air escaping: it was 1N letting out its breath. As Barge said later, when Jo was throwing pretend fainting fits in the playground, 'Never, in the entire history of mankind – *certainly* never in all the time I have been here, and I, I can safely say, have been here quite as long as anyone else, if not a great deal longer – never,' said Barge, swelling slightly, 'has *any*one beaten Gerry in English.'

'I don't quite see it as beaten, exactly.' Jo was anxious to disclaim any competitive intent, at least where exams were concerned. Miss Lloyd had reminded them, only the other day, 'You are not in competition with one another. It's simply a case of every individual doing the best she can.' Naturally, if one's best turned out to be better than anyone else's, it was only human nature to be a little bit pleased; but it was bad manners to gloat.

Barge had no such inhibitions. She gloated quite shamelessly.

'Jam top of English, Jam hitting all those rounders,

162

Jam getting her poem read out in the poetry recital. . . . I think we can safely say,' said Barge, complacently, 'that the Laing Gang has done somewhat better than average.'

'Well, Jammy has,' said Fij.

'Jammy is part of us. Just as *we* are part of Nellie's; in which connection –' Barge puffed out her cheeks, in self-congratulation – 'I think we can also safely say that, what with one thing and another, such as rounders, such as cricket, such as Gerry being certain to come overall top of First Year exams, such as that week when we had no order marks whatsoever at all, I *think* we can safely say that Nellie's will have very little difficulty in knocking those steaming great nits from Sutton's through a hole in the wall.'

'You mean,' said Bozzy, 'you think we might win the Cup?'

Barge rolled her eyes. 'Isn't that what I just said? I put it to you –' she flung out her arms, appealing to Jo – 'how could I have expressed myself any plainer?'

'I suppose you might just have said that you think we might win the Cup,' said Jo.

Fij giggled.

'Of course, one has to remember,' said Barge, 'that one is dealing with very low-grade intelligence. Bozzy, dear, just concentrate and watch my lips . . . Nell-ie's winn-ee Cup-ee. Savv-y?'

Bozzy tapped a knowing finger to her forehead.

'That's right,' said Barge, kindly. 'She's trying to tell you that she's not very bright. She'll understand a bit better tomorrow, when she sees Kay go up on the platform. Until then, it's probably better not to confuse her.'

On Tuesday, in the big hall, the whole school gathered. Miss Durndell presided, standing behind her lectern on the stage, with the four House head mistresses and head prefects seated in a semicircle behind her. First there were prayers to be got through, then Miss Durndell usual end-of-term speech, followed by a whole load of totally boring announcements of no conceivable interest to anyone whatsoever, such as people winning scholarships, and people going abroad and people being awarded exhibitions.

Long before they reached the really important part, the First Years were showing signs of restlessness. (Exhibitions of *what*? wondered Jo. Paintings? But how could you be awarded an exhibition of paintings? Where would you put them all?) It was only when Miss Durndell said, 'And now we come to the Dorothy Beech Cup,' that Barge and Bozzy perked up and sat higher in their seats, and the Bookends stopped playing cat's cradle, and Nadge stopped chewing her finger, and Jo stopped thinking about paintings (they'd be all over the *house*) and started to pay attention.

'I am pleased to say,' said Miss Durndell, 'that all four Houses have managed to distinguish themselves in one way or another during the course of the school year . . . Barbara Bannerman of York, for instance, has had her first book published at the age of sixteen. I hope by next term that we shall have a copy in the Junior School Library. A team from Sutton's won the local schools' Top of the Form; Sutton's also came top of the House league in both Hockey and Tennis.'

Hockey and tennis! Barge huffed, noisily. Hockey and tennis didn't count. It was cricket and rounders that were important, plus netball, in the winter. Nellie's had come top in all of those. Miss Durndell duly announced the fact. She then went on to read out the overall exam results, and the overall order mark totals. Even Barge grew a trifle pink and uncomfortable as Nellie's order mark total was revealed to the busily flapping ears of the rest of the school.

'I shall not go into detailed breakdowns as to which forms have been the worse offenders,' said Miss Durndell, 'but I think they will know who they are. I shall only say that I shall be monitoring the situation next term and shall be looking for improvements in certain quarters.'

From the row behind came a vicious kicking: Katy Wells and her mob. Squalid creatures. Barge and Bozzy ostentatiously moved their chairs forward.

'Finally,' said Miss Durndell, 'the moment I know you've all been waiting for . . . this year's winner of the Cup.'

Bozzy gave a little excited squeak of anticipation and tipped forward on her chair. Barge grabbed her just in time.

'By twenty-three points,' said Miss Durndell, 'this year's winner is Roper's.'

ROPER'S?????????? Bozzy choked and fell off her perch. Barge looked as if she were on the verge of an apoplexy. Even Jo felt a moment of shock. Roper's couldn't win the cup! Roper's were *rubbish*.

'Roper's,' continued Miss Durndell, 'may not seem to have distinguished themselves in any of the more obvious ways –' they hadn't distinguished themselves at *all* – 'but quietly and unobtrusively they have gone about their business, working hard, not drawing attention to themselves, until by dint of sheer persistence they have come out on top. Their behaviour record, incidentally, has been truly excellent. Congratulations to them, and let them be an example to us all!'

Under cover of the applause, Bozzy clambered back on to her chair. She watched, pop-eyed, as the Head Prefect from Roper's stepped forward to receive the Cup.

'Couldn't even *walk* properly!' spluttered Bozzy, later, as the Laing Gang moved in a bunch up Shapcott Road, all strung about with shoe bags and tennis racquets and other end-of-term paraphernalia (including reports in sealed brown envelopes). 'Nearly tripped over her huge great feet and went splat.'

'And *did* you see her *neck*? There was *oodles* of it, all coming out of the top of her dress!'

'It is a bit difficult,' ventured Fij, 'to see where else it could come out of – being as it's a neck.'

'That is not the point: the point is, she looks like a *giraffe*.'

'Yes, and what is more,' said Bozzy, 'she's called Thelma.'

'*Thelma*?'

'Thelma Hoadley.'

'Oh, save me!' Barge staggered drunkenly across the pavement, clutching at herself as she did so.

'They're all called dotty names in that house,' said Bozzy. 'Their games captain is called Elinor Pratt.'

166

'Oh, I can't stand it!' shrieked Barge. 'Elinor Pratt and Thelma Hoadley! Oh, it's too much!'

'It doesn't alter the fact,' said Fij, 'that they won.'

'Only because they had hardly any order marks; not because they actually *did* anything.'

'Can you imagine,' said Bozzy, darting a quick sideways glance at Jo, 'how *boring* they must be?'

'*No* initiative –'

'*No* sense of adventure –'

'Just thoroughly wimpish and dim. I think I can safely say,' said Barge, ruffling herself up, 'that no one could claim that about *us*.'

Fij dug Jo in the ribs. Jo tried not to giggle.

'In any case, the main thing isn't that Roper's won. The main thing,' said Barge, showing her usual splendid sportsmanship, 'the main thing is that Sutton's *lost*.'

'And serve them right,' crowed Bozzy.

'Yes; I fancy it's taken the wind out of *their* sails.'

'Just because they've hogged the Cup for the last four years –'

'They will have to learn,' said Barge, 'that there are other things in life besides winning. Fortunately, we in this House have always been aware of that. We *know* that there are other things in life.'

'Such as, for instance, enjoying oneself,' said Bozzy.

'Such as, for instance, enjoying oneself. You must admit,' said Barge, doing one of her sudden descents from the lofty spheres of philosophy to the somewhat less exalted levels of everyday speech, 'you must admit that we have had fun.'

Bozzy nodded. 'It's been a really, really good term.'

'Yes, it has,' agreed Barge. 'A *really* good term.'

'And we were quite right to vote Jam as form captain.'

'Oh, absolutely!' said Barge. 'A stroke of sheer genius.' She swung her school bag from one shoulder to the other, almost decapitating a passing cyclist as she did so. 'It has to be said,' said Barge, 'we shouldn't have had *nearly* as much fun without Jam.'

Other great reads from **Red Fox**

Further Red Fox titles that you might enjoy reading are listed on the following pages. They are available in bookshops or they can be ordered directly from us.

If you would like to order books, please send this form and the money due to:

ARROW BOOKS, BOOKSERVICE BY POST, PO BOX 29, DOUGLAS, ISLE OF MAN, BRITISH ISLES. Please enclose a cheque or postal order made out to Arrow Books Ltd for the amount due, plus 30p per book for postage and packing to a maximum of £3.00, both for orders within the UK. For customers outside the UK, please allow 35p per book.

NAME _____

ADDRESS _____

_____

Please print clearly.

Whilst every effort is made to keep prices low, it is sometimes necessary to increase cover prices at short notice. If you are ordering books by post, to save delay it is advisable to phone to confirm the correct price. The number to ring is THE SALES DEPARTMENT 071 (if outside London) 973 9700.

Other great reads ← *from* **Red Fox**

Enjoy Jean Ure's stories of school and home life.

JO IN THE MIDDLE

The first of the popular Peter High series. When Jo starts at her new school, she determines never again to be plain, ordinary Jo-in-the-middle.

ISBN 0 09 997730 3   £2.99

FAT LOLLIPOP

The second in the Peter High series. When Jo is invited to join the Laing Gang, she's thrilled – but she also feels guilty because it means she's taking Fat Lollipop's place.

ISBN 0 09 997740 0   £2.99

A BOTTLED CHERRY ANGEL

A story of everyday school life – and the secrets that lurk beneath the surface.

ISBN 0 09 951370 6   £1.99

FRANKIE'S DAD

Frankie can't believe it when her mum marries horrible Billie Small and she has to go and live with him and his weedy son, Jasper. If only her real dad would come and rescue her . . .

ISBN 0 09 959720 9   £1.99

YOU TWO

A classroom story about being best friends – and the troubles it can bring before you find the right friend.

ISBN 0 09 938310 1   £1.95